THE
SIGNAL
FROM
SIRIUS

The Gods of Rapa Nui

ARTHUR C. STAFFORD

ISBN: 978-0-578-71997-9 (sc)
ISBN: 978-1-7923-3553-2 (e)

Because of the dynamic nature of the Internet, any web addresses or
links contained in this book may have changed since publication and
may no longer be valid. The views expressed in this work are solely those
of the author and do not necessarily reflect the views of the publisher,
and the publisher hereby disclaims any responsibility for them.

Any people depicted in stock imagery provided by Getty Images are
models, and such images are being used for illustrative purposes only.
Certain stock imagery © Getty Images.

Scripture taken from the King James Version of the Bible.

Lulu Publishing Services rev. date: 07/31/2020

To Patty

CONTENTS

ACKNOWLEDGEMENTS

This story would not be possible were it not for the hard work and dedication shown by several individuals who deserve special recognition for their contributions. Thank you, Erich von Daniken, who first inspired me with his wondrous tales in *Chariots of the Gods,* and who opened my eyes to the possibilities of extraterrestrial visitations. Thanks to Dr. Jill Tarter for her dedicated work on SETI, the *Search for Extraterrestrial Intelligence* project, and thanks to Dr. Carl Sagan for his great novel—*Contact.* Thanks to Dr. Anne Van Tilberg for her extensive and exhaustive research on Easter Island. Thanks also go to Drs. John D. Kraus and Jerry Ehman for building the *Big Ear* at The Ohio State University. Thanks also go to Dr. John D. Keyser for his analysis of the *Trojan Origins of European Royalty.* I also want to thank Wayanay Inka for their beautiful Peruvian music, and a special thanks to Phil Coulter and to Ronan Tynan for composing and performing one of my favorite songs, *The Town I Loved So Well.* Special thanks to Cindy Foley, who proof-read the manuscript and gave me a tutorial on punctuation and point of view. I would also like to thank the J. C. Penney Company for having the sense of humor to give me a job while in College.

-ACS, Madison, Ohio

EPIGRAPH

I resent the stupid wastefulness of a system which requires that human beings with great labor and pain should spend years in acquiring knowledge, experience and skill, and then just when at last they might use all this in the service of mankind and for their own happiness, they lose their teeth and their hair and their wits, and are hurriedly bundles, together with all that they have learnt, into the grave and nothingness.

It is clear that, if there is a purpose in the universe and a creator, both are unintelligible to us. But that does not provide them with an excuse or a defence....

Leonard Sidney Woolf

CHAPTER 1

THE LETTER

When Larkin first read the letter he thought it was crazy. You couldn't really blame him. Things like this didn't happen in Manhattan. Telecom Communications was a giant conglomerate of electronics, communications and computer firms, whose headquarters was a tall glass and steel monolith on Madison Avenue. Trade journals were currently lauding the merits of their newest creation, the Telecom 770 Integral Computer. This latest evolution in electronic brains was just that. By analyzing the structure of neurons, or nerve cells, in the human brain, scientists were able to duplicate the electrochemical process, and to build tiny electrochemical units capable of carrying on many of the brain's functions. Since computers are not limited to the size of a cranial cavity, it was possible to build a "brain" of almost any size, with infinite memory units, total recall, and the ability to perform any mental function by simply altering its electrochemical circuits.

In short, the Telecom 770 could be modified and adapted to any situation where precise decisions were required: piloting space craft, regulating utilities, deploying weapons, controlling traffic, and keeping the accounts of the thousands of governmental and business concerns. The Telecom 770 was the executive's dream and the C.P.A.'s nightmare.

And the mastermind of all this computerized precision was Dr. Jonas Larkin, Vice President for Research and Development, Telecom Communications, Inc. He held two Ph.D.'s in mathematics and physics from California Institute of Technology, but being a modest man, only wore his Phi Beta Kappa key on formal occasions. He was all business at work, and that long, impressive title was shortened to "Larkin" by his own order. "Dr." was superfluous, and "Jonas" was the exclusive property of his wife, Patty, and a few very select friends.

Larkin was 55 years old, a "young fifty-five" as he liked to put it. He stood just over six feet. He weighed 185 on good days, but if he became engrossed in a project, he would forget regular meals, and his weight would drop as much as twenty pounds. When he weighed himself that morning, he was down to 177. On the other hand, between projects, his appetite would become voracious. Snacking was a constant problem, especially when channel-surfing on the TV. He loved to watch baseball (He had once tried out for the Buffalo Bisons, but an injury to his pitching arm ended any chance of appearing in the Big Leagues.) Jonas would sit in his big, leather recliner watching his giant screen. If two games were on, he'd flip channels using the PIP (Picture in picture) button. Although a resident of New York, Larkin was a native of Ohio. He'd grown up outside Cleveland in a town called Willoughby. His favorite team was the Cleveland Indians, and this led to some heated discussions with his many Yankee fans at work. He kept a cabinet next to his chair, which resembled an honor bar in a hotel. A small refrigerator was filled with beer, soft drinks and mixers. A cabinet above the refrigerator was filled with snacks of every conceivable kind, from nuts to chips to chocolate. Larkin could gain weight as fast as he lost, and his wardrobe reflected the problem. His wife, Patty, who, in addition to her other duties, functioned as his fashion coordinator, was constantly frustrated by his roller-coaster weight problems. She also worried about the effects this had on his health. However, as soon as she warned him, a new project would start, and the weight would go down. It was a never-ending battle. With work nearing completion on the 770, she knew his weight was about to soar again.

Larkin had a full crop of dark brown hair, but his sideburns were graying. He had piercing blue eyes, wore horn-rimmed glasses, and smoked a different pipe from his meerschaum collection once each day. Larkin relished great food, loved travel, and enjoyed great music. Carl Maria von Weber was his favorite composer, and he could remember the smallest details of each of the fourteen performances of *Der Freischuetz* he had seen throughout the world. Jonas Larkin was comfortable, and confident.

As inventor, developer and master of the Telecom 770, Larkin was responsible for all operations, technical inquiries, and the supplying of all data to customers. Like all industries, however, Telecom Communications had to protect itself from industrial espionage, and the actual specifications of the computer were a very closely guarded secret. As a result, all requests for information had to be carefully screened. It was while acting in this capacity that Larkin became aware of the first strange letter.

The letter arrived by registered mail about six weeks after the initial announcement on the computer was made. It was dated June 2, 2001 and postmarked Lima, Peru, but the return address was Pucallpa, a town in eastern Peru. The letter was hand-written. It requested specific information on the maximum mathematical functions of the computer, with particular emphasis on astronomical problems. The letter was signed "Hector Rimirez Villa-Ramos," and Larkin at first dismissed it as an intra-office prank, especially when he read what was written underneath the signature, "Doctor of Mathematics, Massachusetts Institute of Technology, 1991." Somebody had to be playing games. After all, what would a mathematician be doing in a godforsaken place like the rain forests of eastern Peru? And what could he possibly want with the latest computer? This jerk didn't even own a typewriter. It had to be a joke.

Larkin, however, was a scientist as well as a businessman. As a scientist, he could not ignore any possibility, and as a businessman, he could not overlook any potential customer. Besides, there was one sure way to find out if this was a hoax. Call M.I.T. and find out if Hector Rimirez Villa-Ramos had ever attended. A simple phone call to the Records Office, a chat with Fred Hotchkiss, an old friend and classmate, as well as being Registrar, and this whole thing could be easily settled.

As he finished re-reading the letter, Larkin touched his intercom button. "Mrs. Miller," Larkin spoke.

"Yes, Dr. Larkin," came the immediate response. Kate Miller had been Larkin's administrative assistant for nearly ten years. Kate was barely five feet tall, but a real spitfire workaholic, who came to Telecom after leaving the Army. She and her husband were still in the reserves. She always looked immaculate with her closely cropped hair and impeccably manicured nails. Her ready smile belied a keen business sense. Despite her size she made an impressive appearance with her perfectly tailored suits. Larkin often thought that if there were one person more efficient than a computer, it would be Kate. If Larkin was in, so was Kate. His schedule dictated hers, with but one exception three years earlier. Kate was absent for six weeks for the birth of her daughter.

"Could you check your Rolodex for a Fred Hotchkiss at MIT, and get him on the line for me, please?"

"Right away, sir." Larkin tolerated her formality with him

because he knew it made *her* feel important. Besides, it promoted a positive image with strangers.

Larkin continued looking at the letter. Although written on a yellow legal pad, the handwriting was neat and deliberate. There was not a single correction or misspelled word on any of the pages. It reminded him of Mozart. Once the great composer set his music on paper it never needed changes.

"Dr. Larkin," Mrs. Miller's voice broke his thought, "Fred Hotchkiss on line one."

"Thank you," Larkin responded, touching the conference call button.

"Hello, Fred? This is Jonas Larkin."

"Jonas Larkin!" Fred answered from the other end. "Long time no see. How've you been doing?"

"Fine."

"Fine. Is that all you can say? Listen, old friend, Massachusetts isn't the end of the world. How about visiting us once in a while? We know all about that new computer you've dreamed up. I could arrange some lecture time for you, perhaps even a get-away to my place up in Maine."

"Sounds great, Fred. Perhaps after I wind things up here. Patty wants me to spend some time with her and the kids first, but maybe afterwards...."

"How is Patty?" Fred interrupted

"She's fine, too. Listen, Fred, I wonder if you could do me a favor?"

"Sure, Jonas, only what do you need me for? What do you need anybody for, except maybe to replace the hamster on the wheel of that new brain you've built."

"Very funny. Look, I want you to check on a name for me. He's applied for a job here, and he lists M.I.T. as his school. I need to know all about him. You know what I mean?"

"Sure. What's his name, anyway?"

"You've probably never heard of him. Got a pencil?"

"Sure do. Shoot."

"O.K. It's Hector Rimirez..."

"Wait a minute, Jonas, you don't mean to tell me you've got Hector Rimirez Villa-Ramos?"

"Why, do you *know* him?"

"Know him! Jonas, this guy's a prodigy, a real genius. He got his doctorate at seventeen. We couldn't teach him enough. He took every upper level course we had in math, physics, chemistry and history. History fascinated him. He really got interested in early American culture, those Indian tribes that lived in Mexico and Peru. He lives in Peru. The last we heard from him he'd gone back down there to do some kind of research. What did he do? Give up and come back here to work for you?"

"Not exactly," Larkin said, in utter disbelief, "he's interested in my computer."

"Well, that figures. Ours were no match for him. 'Not good enough' he would say. Well, all I can say is if you get a chance to hire him, *do* it. He's a good one."

"Yes, thanks," Larkin said, still not believing.

"Well," Hotchkiss said, "Don't forget what I said about my place in Maine. Harriet would love to see you two again. Let me know if you need anything else, and give my best to Patty."

"I will, Fred, and thanks again."

"Anytime, Jonas—bye now."

"Bye, Fred."

Larkin slowly touched the conference call button. "How about that?" Jonas thought. "It wasn't a joke."

He dictated a response as best he could, without divulging any company secrets. Call it professional jealousy, but deep inside, Larkin almost wished that Villa-Ramos would find his computer inadequate. Mrs. Miller did her usual job of polishing the prose,

6

and correcting Jonas's errors. Unlike Villa-Ramos, Jonas' hand-writing was atrocious. The letter went out the following day. Larkin wondered if he would even get a response.

He didn't have long to wait.

The second letter was printed on stationery belonging to the Hotel Libertador in Lima, and used the hotel as a return address. Apparently, Villa-Ramos' fortunes had improved somewhat.

"I sincerely apologize," the letter read, "for not using proper business etiquette in my initial communication, but it was very urgent that I inquire as to the precision of your Telecom 770. My research has progressed to a point where I require a computer of extreme accuracy. Unfortunately, much of my work must be done in remote areas, and I had not the time to compose my correspon-dence in a more formal framework.

"The general description which you have generously provided indicates that this machine could be the type I need. In any case, it is well worth seeing. I shall be arriving in New York as soon as transportation can be arranged.

Larkin was becoming more and more puzzled. What did Villa-Ramos have in mind?

Two days later Larkin had a partial answer. The newspapers were filled with the story. A huge treasure had recently been un-earthed in a valley on the leeward side of the Peruvian Andes. Millions of dollars in gold, silver and precious stones had been found. Statuettes, jewelry, ingots and other artifacts had been hidden in a previously unrecorded site. By careful study and anal-ysis of some newly discovered ancient inscriptions, a Dr. Hector Rimirez Villa-Ramos was able to pinpoint the location. He was donating the treasure to the Peruvian government at a fraction of its total worth, in order to finance "further explorations" in the area.

Larkin was astounded. Could these "future explorations" pos-sibly involve him? The next bombshell came in the form of a phone call from the Peruvian Consulate in New York. Mrs. Miller, in her usual precise manner had recorded the message exactly as she heard it. The Peruvians, she wrote, wished to send a representative to confer with Dr. Larkin on "an unusual and large financial transaction to be conducted between the Government of the Republic of Peru, on behalf of Dr. Hector Rimirez Villa-Ramos, and Telecom Communications, Inc." This representative, a member of the consulate staff, would accompany Dr. Villa-Ramos to the conference. The ground rules were simple, but absolute. Only the three men would be present, along with a prototype of the new computer. The meeting would take place in Larkin's private office, with all means of external communication "disengaged."

Six days later, at 11 a.m., Mrs. Miller received a second message, which she dutifully recorded. Reached by beeper, Larkin was immediately informed that Dr. Hector Villa-Ramos had arrived in New York at 10 a.m. that morning and was meeting with officials at the Peruvian Consulate. These included members of the Peruvian delegation to the United Nations. Larkin was asked if he could arrange a meeting for 2 o'clock p.m. on Tuesday, the following day.

"Mrs. Miller," Larkin replied. "Tell them, 'By all means,' and clear my calendar for the rest of the day. I don't know how long this will take."

"Certainly, sir, and should I put Wednesday on hold, as well?"

"Yes, perhaps you should," Larkin answered. Something told him this was going to be a very long meeting.

CHAPTER II

THE MEETING

A t precisely 1:55 p.m. the following day, a consulate limousine pulled in front of the Telecom Communications and two men arrived for their two o'clock appointment.

Jonas was at once eager and apprehensive. The whole thing was so incredible and mysterious. Who could have guessed that a hand-written letter could mushroom into this?

"Dr. Larkin," Mrs. Miller buzzed, "Dr. Villa-Ramos and Mr. Delgado from the Peruvian consulate."

"Show them in, Mrs. Miller."

"Yes, Doctor."

The door opened. Mrs. Miller ushered them in quickly, and left the room. Jonas knew that their privacy was assured. Mrs. Miller would see to that. Security was fully aware of the situation, and emergency hotlines were in place to alert authorities of any breach. Furthermore, as Mrs. Miller had reminded Larkin on several occasions, "I've got a black belt in case anyone makes trouble." Larkin thought she was joking at first, but later had second thoughts. "She probably does," he thought. He had never known her to lie about anything.

"Gentlemen, this is a real pleasure," said Larkin, extending his hand to Villa-Ramos. "I've really been looking forward to this ever since I received that first letter."

"Thank, you, Doctor"

"Skip the formalities. The name is Jonas."

"Fine. Well in that case, my name is Hector. In school everyone called me 'Hec' as in 'What the....'"

"Hec it is then," Jonas replied jokingly, although he was burning inside. The man standing in front of him, shaking his hand, was only twenty-five. Larkin could already sense that he was outclassed.

Hector was struck immediately with the size and opulence of Larkin's office. It reflected perfectly the status Dr. Larkin held in the company. It was a walnut paneled affair, measuring approximately thirty feet by thirty feet square, having the prerequisite corner view of the Manhattan skyline, which was spectacular from the fortieth floor. In addition to all the usual accoutrements such an office dictated there was an enormous glass case extending along an entire wall. Inside that case was a veritable museum of telecommunications devices. There was a Berliner disc phonograph with Nipper listening to "His Master's Voice®", an Edison cylinder phonograph, an early Western Union® telegraph key and receiver, and an antique Bell® telephone. There was also a Philco® table radio and an Underwood® typewriter from the 1920's, an RCA Victor® radio-phonograph console from the late 1940's, a Crosley® twelve-inch black and white television from 1950. A Burroughs® adding machine, a 1970's Radio Shack® pocket calculator, a Lear® 8-track tape player, and a Commodore 64 personal computer from the early 1980's. There was even a dial telephone with Mickey Mouse® holding the receiver. Hector surmised that these items were collected by Jonas either as things he actually used, or as items acquired as he traveled to various flea markets and antique shows over the years.

However, what struck Hector most was a framed news article hanging inside the case. It was dated December 12, 1971, and its author was a young college student named Jonas Larkin. It read as follows:

PROGRESS IS OUR MOST IMPORTANT PROBLEM

"Machines were invented to make our lives more carefree and enjoyable. They help us build our houses and live in our houses. They help us build our factories and work in our factories. They help us earn our salaries, and they are most adept at taking our salaries. Every week millions of Americans pick up their computerized paychecks from computerized paymasters, and go to their computerized banks to deposit their salaries in computerized accounts so they can make out computerized checks to pay their computerized bills.

"This modern system works great until one of those computers goes haywire. Then, friend, you have a problem. Our machines are the most conceited things in the world. They are never wrong, and trying to argue with an IBM® machine is like talking to a meat grinder. Your language can be as eloquent as filet mignon, or as harsh as a dried-out soup bone; the computer doesn't care. It all comes out as hamburger in the end, and as far as the computer is concerned, hamburger is hamburger.

"Little cards with numbers and holes: the hamburger of life. I heard of a guy who walked to his mailbox one day, and pulled out a bill from the Gas Company. On the bill was printed the following: 'Balance due $0.00.' The man promptly threw the bill in the wastebasket. The next month, however, he received a Second Notice, which read: 'Please remit $0.00. Disregard this notice if you have already paid.' Again, he threw the bill away. Now the computer was becoming ornery. 'Please forward payment immediately, or we shall be forced to discontinue service,' the Final Notice read, between the dots, dashes and holes.

"Angered by this threat, the customer thought two could play at this game, so he wrote out a check for $0.00 and sent it to the Gas Company. The following week he received this reply: 'Thank you,' the computerized note read, 'for your prompt payment.'

"You might think it ended there, but never underestimate the power of a computer. The very next day he customer received a computerized letter from his bank, informing him that his check for $0.00 had bounced because he didn't have $0.00 in his account!

"Sooner or later each of us meets a computer that is out to get us. I have already met mine. It resides at the Columbia® Stereo Tape Club in Terre Haute, Indiana. For the past three months I have been putting up with its antics waiting for someone to fix it. For the last three months the computer has been trying to get someone to fix me.

"It all started when I returned a defective tape entitled 'The Ventures Knock Me Out', and demanded a replacement, which the club guarantees in these instances. Apparently, the computer disliked the additional paperwork and was determined to get paid for its time. When I received my replacement tape, I also received a bill for $8.64. I returned the bill with a letter in which I explained that the tape had already been paid for. The computer disliked apologizing even more, but at last it conceded that the bill 'should be considered as a mailing slip only.'

"A word to the wise: never force a computer to apologize. Today, I opened my front door. A large box was sitting on the step. It contained ten Lawrence Welk tapes and a bill for $86.40!

Hector had become so engrossed in the display that he forgot that there were other people in the room. Turning from the article,

Hector, slightly flushed, said "Please forgive me, uh, Jonas, this is Cesar Delgado of the Peruvian Embassy."

"Pleased to make your acquaintance, too," Larkin said, as they shook hands. Delgado reminded Larkin of a character right out of Dickens—a bank clerk, or bookkeeper, perhaps. Bob Cratchit with a Spanish accent, five feet, eight inches tall, slightly pudgy, with dark, almost black hair, wearing a black suit and carrying the quintessential briefcase.

"Likewise, I'm sure," Delgado responded.

"Cesar is here to arrange the finances," Hector said, "but that will come later. Right now, I'm anxious to see this computer first hand."

"Certainly," Larkin said, leading them into his private work-shop behind the office.

"I couldn't help admiring your collection," Hector said. "I take it from the article that you weren't always fond of computers, Jonas."

"Not fond of bad ones, or bad programming," Larkin replied, as he began sizing up his young friend. Hector was strikingly handsome. Slightly shorter than Larkin, he was very well built, with a dark complexion, long, straight black hair and penetrating brown eyes. His smile belied a cool, confident attitude—not quite arrogance—but close. His handclasp was very firm, and it was obvious that he spent much of his time outdoors. The suit he wore was not a tailored fit, and he looked out of place in it. Hector was a born dominator. Larkin could sense this. Larkin was usually the master at controlling situations, but this young man had beaten him to the punch already.

"So, this is it," Hector said, as they stepped up to the machine. "Beautiful."

"That's hardly the word," Larkin thought to himself as Hector began scrutinizing the intricate device. Larkin had been in com-puters almost since Hector was born. Even as a small boy he had been fascinated with electronics. He recalled that the only time his father ever struck him was because of an "experiment" he tried. As a boy, Jonas was a very inquisitive child. He always wanted to know what made everything work. As a result, he was constantly taking things apart, which caused no end of aggravation for his parents. One day, at the age of ten, Jonas was watching TV in the living room. It was 1962 and color television was a relatively new invention. His parents had recently purchased a large console color TV at a cost of nearly $1000, a great deal of money at that time. They had placed it next to the console radio and phonograph— sort of an early version of a home entertainment center. As Jonas watched the TV, one of those late afternoon musical shows came on, featuring hits by the latest teen idol. He couldn't remember if it was Bobby Vee or Paul Anka, but it was one that his older sister, Ruthie was crazy about. She had all his records.

As Jonas watched, he was suddenly struck by a fabulous idea. Why not plug the phonograph into the television set. That way, by playing the record, one could watch the singer at the same time. It was brilliant!

Mom was busy making dinner in the kitchen. Ruthie was talking on the phone in her room, and probably would be for hours. Jonas saw his chance. Grabbing a screwdriver from Dad's workbench, Jonas crawled behind both units. Disconnecting the antenna leads from the television first, Jonas next traced the wires leading from the amplifier on the radio to the speakers. He connected the speaker wires to the antenna leads. Next he took out a record from the storage cabinet of the console and placed it on the record changer. Then, with a smile on his face, he turned on the radio.

A very loud "pop!" was followed by smoke wafting from behind the television set, along with the distinct odor of ozone. Instead of a picture, the screen was dark. Mom came running from the kitchen. Jonas was in a state of shock, literally and figuratively. She quickly pulled the plugs, and rescued her son from certain disaster. However, an even larger one awaited him when father came home.

Jonas loved to tell that story. "Today," he would say, jokingly. "CD's and DVD's are commonplace. I was just forty years ahead of my time."

Yes, Jonas had truly been a pioneer in computers and telecommunications. He'd helped to design and build the finest systems in existence. There was nothing about computers that Jonas Larkin didn't know. He'd show this young upstart a thing or two.

For hours the two scientists poured over the specifications, schematic diagrams, and sample problems. As his academic history showed, Hector seemed to grasp every concept with ease. The two men became so involved that they completely forgot about time, and about Mr. Delgado, who eventually dozed off from boredom.

"This is it," Hector summarized, after digesting all the information Jonas could give him. "This is the computer I need."

"I see," said Larkin, "and just exactly what is it that you need this computer for?"

"My research. If I'm right, mankind is about to make the greatest discovery in its history, and your computer, Jonas, is the tool by which that discovery is going to be made."

"What in God's name are you talking about?" Jonas asked.

"An excellent choice of words, Jonas," Hector said, "It may very well be."

"May very well be what?"

"In God's name."

The student was now lecturing the teacher, and the lecture Villa-Ramos gave filled Jonas with wonder and apprehension. What Hector proposed to do with Larkin's computer was beyond anything Larkin could ever have imagined. The story was so fantastic, that if anyone other than a man of Villa-Ramos' reputation had told it, Larkin would immediately have dismissed it as the ravings of a lunatic. But Hector was no lunatic, and his sincerity was genuine.

As Larkin understood it, this was Hector's theory:

Many centuries ago, before Europeans even knew there was an America, highly advanced and complex civilizations had developed in what we call Central and South America.

The Mayans, who lived in what was now southern Mexico, the Mayan Peninsula, and Guatemala, Reached their zenith at about 1000 AD. They designed and built elaborate stone temples, and pyramids rivaling those in Egypt. They learned to breed corn from wild grass. They developed an accurate calendar based on precise astronomical observations, and their numbering system was similar to Arabic, far superior to the Roman.

The Aztecs, who conquered the Mayans, had physicians and surgeons comparable to the best in contemporary Europe. They spread an empire throughout central Mexico. Their capital, Tenochtitlan, located where Mexico City presently stands, boasted a population of over one hundred thousand. Few cities in the contemporary world were larger.

Farther south, in the Andes of Peru, the Incas ruled one of the largest empires in all history. Their builders and stone cutters were so precise that gigantic rocks, weighing many tons each, could be made to fit together so exactly that light would not shine between them, and mortar was not needed. From their capital, Cuzco, they built thousands of miles of paved roads, yet the Incas had no wheels. They also carved stones, which resembled conduits, yet there was no evidence that they had plumbing. They carved huge figures, which could only be appreciated from the air, and they designed fields, which seemed to resemble landing strips when seen from high altitudes. Obviously, the Incas could not fly, so why did they consume so much time and energy working on projects they seemingly couldn't use afterwards?

Other places in the world also offered similar mysteries. Consider Stonehenge in England. How could men, possessed of only hand tools, possibly build such a formation? They would have had to haul gigantic stones over long distances, for no quarries existed nearby. They also had to lift them into place, yet they knew nothing of blocks and tackles, or pulleys, and there is no evidence of inclined planes, either. More importantly, why was it necessary to build the formation in *this* location, rather than next to a quarry? What was so special about this place?

But, probably the greatest mystery of all was the stone statues on Easter Island. The rock was so hard that primitive tools could barely cut it. And, even if it were possible to cut the stone, Easter Island was so barren that it could hardly support the thousands of laborers that such a project would have required. What did they eat? Where did they live? How did they cut the volcanic rock, and then raise each statue to stare forever up into the sky? More importantly, why did they do it? What force was driving them?

The Egyptian civilization offered still more mystery. Why did the pharaohs command tens of thousands of laborers and slaves to build the great pyramids of Giza. Were they just tombs for the royal rulers, or did they serve some other purpose? Was it mere coincidence that the configuration of the three pyramids was an exact duplicate of the configuration of the three stars comprising the belt of the constellation Orion? Could it be that the pharaohs wanted to contact someone out there, someone they might meet in the next life?

Even the Israelites, who served as slaves under the pharaohs, were not immune. In Job, Chapter 38, God described how powerful He is by questioning Job, "Can you hold back the Stars? Can you restrain Orion or Pleiades? Can you ensure the proper sequence of the seasons, or guide the constellation of the Bear with her satellites across the heavens? Do you know the laws of the universe and how the heavens influence the earth?" Of all the constellations in the heavens, why did God choose Orion as an example?

All these cultures have one thing in common. They believed that their god, or gods, resided in heaven, or space. Many of their idols resemble spacemen in appearance.

Finally, Hector had concluded his theory with this pronouncement, "I believe that at some remote time in the past we were visited by creatures, 'gods', from outer space."

Jonas still couldn't believe what Hector had told him. This man, this brilliant scientist, actually believed in "little green men." Incredible. Preposterous.

"You mean to stand there and tell me you believe in this theory?"

"Yes, I do," Hector said, "but I can see you don't."

"Doctor," Larkin shot back, "you are aware that science requires proof. Speculation isn't good enough. Even quoting the Bible doesn't help unless you can prove it. I can't believe that a man of your intelligence could get sucked into this Erich von Daniken stuff, this *Chariots of the Gods* crap."

"You're familiar with Daniken, then?" Hector asked.

"Of course I am. It was fun to read. But it's not science. Its speculation, and shaky speculation at that. Where's the proof, Doctor—the proof?"

"Well, to begin with," said Hector, "I have found El Dorado."

"El Dorado?" Larkin asked, dumbfounded. "What do you mean you have found El Dorado?"

"Surely you've heard the legend," Hector replied. "You must have read the news stories on my discovery. Where do you think the money came from to buy your computer?"

Larkin sat down. "Let me get this straight," he said. "You actually believed an old Spanish wives' tale about a lost city of gold, so you just went out there in the jungle and dug it up! You're not even an archaeologist. How come you found it, and they couldn't?"

"For the same reason I need your computer," Hector replied, "Mathematics. By studying the ancient inscriptions and glyphs, I was able to piece together a mathematical model, which would allow me to make and decipher maps much like the ancients did. Finding El Dorado using that model proved I was right. You see, Jonas—May I still call you that?"

"Certainly."

"Thank you. You see, Jonas, if my theory, and Daniken's for that matter, is correct, there has to be a second similarity in all these phenomena. Not only did each of these cultures believe in 'gods from outer space', as Daniken would call them, but they also had to have an identical and logical mathematical system. Mathematics is the only truly infinite concept found throughout the universe. Everything that happens, whether it is physical, chemical or biological, can be explained in mathematical terms. We know that these cultures were capable of making accurate calendars, excellent maps, and astronomical charts. They were able to move tremendous weights over long distances, which implies knowledge of physics and engineering, some of which we still can't duplicate. Did you know that one tribe, the Olmecs, could transport and dress stones weighing a hundred tons each. How could they do that? It's nearly impossible for us to do it today! Why, for example, did the Incas cultivate cotton three thousand feet above sea level? They had no use for it. They didn't have any looms! Or, maybe, they weren't growing the cotton for themselves at all. They were growing it for someone else. I am convinced, Jonas, that these cultures were started by, and relied upon, extraterrestrial help."

"Hector—er—Hec," Jonas asked, "Do you fully realize the implication of that statement? You are saying that mankind's development was much more than mere coincidence. You're saying that an intelligent civilization from somewhere in space came here, took us under its wing, so to speak, and taught us the basics. Then, it left us alone to advance on that framework?"

"That and more," Hector resumed. "I believe that *that* intelligence is out there still. I believe that these ancient civilizations did not merely believe that their 'gods' were coming back. They expected it. They were so convinced of it that every endeavor, every day of their lives, was spent in preparation for a return, which never came...or is yet to come. The landing strips, the observatories, the paved roads, the applications of physics and biology, the careful preservation of mathematics—it all points that way. None of these civilizations understood the concept of flight, but the abundance of it in their art certainly indicates to me that they knew someone who did—someone who needed landing strips, conduits, paved roads, accurate astronomy, and logical numbers. Perhaps the Incas, the Egyptians, the Aztecs and the others, were awaiting the return of their 'sun god'. He would descend from Heaven in a ball of fire, a flaming chariot like Ezekiel describes in the Old Testament, and set down on the landing strip, travel the paved roads in his thunder cart, and pass judgment on his people—perhaps to make them gods like himself."

"Incredible," Larkin said, "but, if these civilizations were so civilized, why the human sacrifices? Why the wars?"

"Call them mistakes, or better yet, miscalculations," Hector replied. "After a long period of time, when the 'gods' hadn't returned, each of these cultures tried to contact them. Offering a human sacrifice would have been a logical approach for people lacking radio or laser beams with which to probe space. Perhaps by offering one of their own, one of their finest specimens, they hoped to appease the 'sun god', and to bring him back. This would also explain the Egyptians' preoccupation with death. The Egyptians revered their pharaohs in life as being equal with the gods. Accordingly, when a pharaoh died, it was believed that his spirit would join the gods through his preserved body. Hence, the elaborate ceremonies. Boats were even buried along with the dead monarchs so that they could use them to journey to the other gods in the heavens. What better way to express mathematical accuracy and engineering know-how than to build a structure as massive and complex as a pyramid—the ultimate sacrifice."

"And wars?" Larkin added.

"Well," Hector continued, "when these aliens came to Earth, they couldn't be absolutely sure that their plan would work. So, in order to improve the odds, they started several different colonies at remote places on the planets' surface—Egypt, Central America, China—sort of like planting several bacterial cultures on a sterile petri dish. They couldn't be sure which would survive, but they more or less had an equal chance." "Math?" Larkin interrupted.

"Yes, as well as some basic applications and tools. They started with the basic aboriginal man, which they found here, and by careful breeding, over a period of several thousand years, were able to develop the early cultures. Naturally, successful cultures would compete with each other for control of the planet, and it is this inherited competitiveness, which later evolved into wars between the competing societies.

"It's my belief that the aliens thought that eventually these battles would end, and that one super-vigorous hybrid would emerge to completely dominate the world. Take the Chachapoyas, for example.

"The who?" Larkin asked.

"Forgive me," Hector replied. "When you've studied these people for as long as I have, you think that everyone else has heard of them as well. The Chachapoyas were a tribe of tall, fair-skinned warriors who lived in eastern Peru at the time of the Incas. The Incas conquered them shortly before the Spanish conquest. They were such good fighters, however, that the Inca nobility used them as bodyguards. In 2000, an American explorer, Gene Savoy discovered the lost city of Cajamarquilla, one of their settlements dating to about 700 AD. Earlier, he also discovered their capital, Gran Vilaya. He has been studying the Chachapoyas for more than forty years. The Chachapoyas and the Incas were competing for the same territory. Eventually, the Incas prevailed, only to be conquered by the Spaniards."

"Sort of 'survival of the fittest'" Larkin concluded.

"Precisely," Hector said. "Unfortunately, we're still fighting. The experiment has not yet proved successful, and you know what happens in the petri dish when all the cultures grow as large as they can.

"Yes," Larkin said, "they all die, killed off by the waste products of their own metabolism."

"Exactly, Jonas, unless they can be rescued. Unless the lab technician separates the cultures, and transfers each of them to a separate, new and sterile culture dish, where they can grow unmolested."

"Agreed, Hec," Larkin said, "but what is your point?"

"It's obvious," Hector retorted, "Don't you see? The Earth is like the crowded petri dish. The experiment is not working. A dominant strain has not emerged. We still fight among ourselves, and our numbers increase so rapidly that food, water, and even the air we breathe, will eventually run out. We will drown in our own excrement. Unless we leave this planet, and colonize new ones, we're all going to die here."

"Oh, come now, Hec," Larkin laughed. "You're being way too pessimistic. Malthus died in 1834, and we've increased several billion since then. Surely we'll find a way to endure. After all, look at what we've accomplished...."

"Everything we've accomplished," Hector interrupted, "has been geared toward one ultimate goal—contacting, and communing with, our creators. Our entire history is an attempt to please them in whatever form we perceive them to be. But, for some reason, our creators haven't heard us. Jonas, I think that the reason they haven't heard us is because, until now, we weren't advanced enough to communicate with them."

"And now we are?"

"Yes, thanks to your computer."

"But," said Jonas, "forgive me if I'm wrong—but isn't someone else already working on this? I recall hearing about it. SETI I think it's called.

"You mean 'Search for Estraterrestrial Intelligence'—Jill Tarter's work"

"Yes," said Jonas. "Come to think of it, there was a movie about that in the mid-nineties—*Contact*—I think it was called."

"Yes, based on a Carl Sagan book," said Hector, "but my project differs significantly."

"How so?" Larkin asked.

"SETI searches all over the universe for signals which might signify alien intelligence. They've been at it for years, and if they succeed it will truly be the greatest discovery in the history of mankind. I wish them well, but the odds are against them."

"How much?" Larkin asked.

"A million to one at least." Hector answered immediately.

"And yours are better?" Larkin quipped.

"Considerably better," Hector replied, "because I'm not looking all over the universe. I have a specific site in mind. Furthermore, unlike SETI, I propose a two-way conversation. First, using your computer, we send a message out there. Then we wait for an answer. Quite simple, really.

"And you are quite certain about this 'specific site'?" Larkin asked, knowing the answer.

"Quite certain," Hector replied.

There was a long silence. Larkin had to compose his thoughts. He couldn't decide whether Hector was merely overreacting, or totally insane. He decided to pursue the matter further.

"All right," he said at last, "If Fred Hotchkiss hadn't vouched for you, I'd swear you were one sandwich short of a picnic."

"A what?" Hector asked.

"Nothing," Larkin replied. "Just a figure of speech." Then Larkin continued, "Listen, if all that you say is true, why do you need my computer? Why don't you go up to the top floor and jump off? Didn't you say earlier that there's no hope for any of us here anyway?"

"That's right," Hector answered deliberately, "I did say that. There may not be any hope for us—here."

"And just exactly what does that mean?" Larkin asked, rather disgustedly.

"What I mean, Jonas—"

"Better make that 'Larkin' for now, or better yet, Dr. Larkin. According to you, I don't have much time left, so I better use the title now while I've still got it."

"All right, *Doctor* Larkin, what I mean is this. Suppose the experiment as I've described it, is not going well. And, suppose that those aliens, who thought the whole thing up in the first place, are still out there, waiting to see how it turns out?"

"Oh, brother," Larkin sighed in disbelief, "of all the crackbrained ideas. Are you sure you have a Ph.D. from M.I.T.? He paused momentarily, and then continued, "OK, *Doctor* Villa-Ramos, if those aliens are still out there, how come they never came back, like the ancients thought they would? How come they aren't helping us now, if we're in as much trouble as you say we are?"

"Simple, Doctor," Hector explained, "because I don't believe that they ever intended to come back!"

"But, you just said...."

"I *said*, Dr. Larkin, that the ancients expected their gods to return. They expected it because the aliens told them that before they left. Tell me, Doctor, haven't you ever made a promise that you had no intention of keeping?"

"I suppose so; but, why would they do it?"

"Incentive."

"Incentive?"

"Certainly. When you want someone to do something, to achieve a certain goal, what do you do? Offer them a bribe, right?"

"Reward sounds better."

"All right, 'reward'. 'Honor me, and keep my commandments, and I shall prepare a place in Heaven for you. You will sit on the right hand of God.' Does that sound familiar?"

"Of course it does," Larkin replied. "In other words, what you're saying is that once the experiment started, and the reward offer was made, the aliens stood back to see what would happen."

"Right. Their promise to return was a hoax. It gave mankind a purpose, something to strive for—the perfect life that each of us wishes for, that all of us work for, but never quite attain."

"I must say, Doctor," Larkin said, "you're a pretty good con artist yourself. But, tell me, you still haven't answered the second part of my question. If we have all this trouble; if the experiment isn't going according to plan, how come they haven't realized it, and come to our aid?"

"That, Doctor, is precisely why I'm here. 'If the mountain won't come to Mohammed....'"

"You're going to try to contact *them*! With my computer!" Larkin yelled. "You must be mad!"

"Doctor, believe me, I almost wish I were."

"And the Peruvians? Delgado. Where is Delgado?"

They both turned, and looked into the office, where Delgado had fallen asleep in one of the chairs. "The world could be ending, and all Peru can do about it is take a nap," Hector said, as he resumed his presentation.

"After calculating the location of the treasure, and finding it, I donated it to the Peruvian Government on the condition that they would supply me with the necessary equipment to do further research. They agreed. They are here to buy one of your computers for my personal use, along with any other equipment I desire. A transmitter and generators will be required, of course."

"But what are you going to do with the computer once you have it?" Larkin asked.

"I am going to talk to the aliens in the one language I hope they understand—mathematics. For years I have been cataloging every inscription the ancients have left behind, scouring the Earth for clues. It was while I was doing this that I stumbled upon an ancient text, which led me to El Dorado. I studied these inscriptions and tried to find a mathematical relationship. There had to be one, and I found it. Then, by applying this relationship to their stone structures, and their observatories, I was able to locate that part of the universe where the aliens originated—the goal toward which all human endeavors have been, perhaps unknowingly, directed. With your computer, I will be able to transmit our human condition into mathematical equations, based upon universal physical, chemical and biological laws. I will transmit this mathematical statement to them, and they will understand it. They must understand. Mankind is not just another experiment—not just another petri dish to be thrown away. We must be saved."

CHAPTER III

THE MISSION

The silence in the room was deafening. Hector was staring at Larkin. Had he convinced him? Larkin was deep in thought. If valid, Hector's theory would become the most monumental discovery in history. If false, there would be no harm done, for no one as yet knew the full impact of his work. Since the legitimate government of a western country was acting as purchasing agent for the computer, Telecom was safe from ridicule in the event that the theory exploded, and was made public. However, doubts remained. The whole idea was so utterly fantastic. Larkin had read Daniken's book, and like most scientists, had dismissed it as unscientific entertainment. To be sure, what Daniken proposed was what many wanted to hear. All those U.F.O. watchers and believers in extraterrestrials had found a champion. What's more, even if logical explanations other than Daniken's could be found for all these phenomena, they still wouldn't disprove his theory. And, most intriguing of all was the fact that Daniken could only speculate; he had no actual proof. Hector, on the other hand, was offering proof—a scientific means of settling the issue once and for all. It was a challenge, which Larkin couldn't ignore, and an excellent way to test his computer under maximum stress.

"Very well, Doctor—er—Hector, I'm not going to say I agree with your theory, but if you've got the money, I've got the time. I'll agree to the sale on one condition."

"And that is?" Hector asked.

"That I accompany you to Peru, with the equipment; that I take charge of the computer programming; that I be permitted to observe your work as a trusted colleague, and that you will agree to make any and all findings public, even if the project is a failure."

"Boy," said Hector, "if that's one condition, I'm glad you didn't have a list." He paused "All right. Welcome aboard, Dr. Larkin."

"The name is Jonas. Shall we drink to it. There's some scotch in my office."

"Great. We better wake up Delgado. There's a lot of work to do."

They stepped back into Larkin's office, woke up their drowsy consulate member, and made a toast to their agreement. After the papers were signed, Mr. Delgado returned to the consulate, and Jonas and Hector remained to iron out the details. Jonas would take an extended leave of absence in order to work in Peru. He had close connections with Consolidated Electric, and they could provide any generators or transmitters needed. The laser was another matter.

"That laser could be a problem," Larkin said, as he relaxed with a meerschaum bearing an elk's head on the bowl.

"Not with the help of the Peruvian Government," Hector responded. "The U.N. is building a new observatory in Peru. It's nearing completion. As part of the settlement for the treasure, I merely convinced them that it might be necessary to use the observatory occasionally in order to check the accuracy of ancient astronomical findings."

"I take it this observatory has a laser?" Larkin asked.

"Of course. The largest in the world, thanks to a generous donation from the United States. They plan to use it for practically the same purpose we are—to communicate over long distances. They also have a large transmitting station for sending signals through space."

"What's the other transmitter for, then?" asked Larkin.

"To communicate with the observatory. You see, it will be necessary to install the computer at my laboratory near Pucallpa. The observatory is located near Huancayo, about two hundred miles away, high in the Andes. We'll need to transmit directly from the computer to the laser device and the transmitter at the observatory."

"Why so far away? Why not install the computer at the observatory?"

"Because all the data I have on the ancients has been stored at Pucallpa. It would take weeks to move it all. I've collected rocks, artifacts, statues, and countless items weighing many tons. Besides, the finest of the ancient observatories is located nearby. We'll need it to verify data. There's also the element of privacy. At Pucallpa we can do all the preliminary work without being disturbed."

"I wasn't aware that there were any Inca ruins located in that area," Larkin said.

"Neither was anyone else until I discovered El Dorado. In 1532, when Pizarro conquered the Incas, several hundred of their most learned priests and scholars took a large treasure and escaped over the Andes into the western Amazon. There they found refugees from the Aztec Empire, who had fled south earlier. They settled along the Ucayali and Yavari rivers, and re-established a culture, which I call 'Mayatec' because of the similarities in architecture. These scholars kept all the ancient records of their two cultures, including those of the Olmecs, Mayas and Toltecs, which had been handed down for generations. They built temples, observatories and sacrificial altars to their gods, but there was no answer. Apparently, the colony was wiped out by an epidemic, and the rainforest reclaimed its lost territory. When I arrived, it was impossible to tell that anyone ever had lived there. The pyramids looked like tree-covered hills, and the records and treasures were buried under them. It was only by the most careful research that I happened to find the right place."

"Yes, but how did you find out the location of El Dorado from the artifacts?" Larkin asked.

"From a buried tablet I found in one of the temples at Tiahuanaco. Apparently, in their haste to leave, these Incas felt a need to return to the ancient city, and leave a message. That was what really got me started. Why would the Incas bother to leave a message in a ruined city, a city so old that they didn't even know its origin? Obviously, they believed that someone would return to Tiahuanaco in the future, and would need to know how to get to the new settlement.

"When I finally made the discovery, not only did I find treasure, but also a wealth of tablets containing countless inscriptions, including an exact copy of the inscription on the great Idol of Tiahuanaco, which contains a huge amount of astronomical data. However, the most fantastic discovery of all was a gold, jeweled case containing a scroll. The scroll was made of papyrus, and it told the story of a great flood. It was of Egyptian origin! Heyerdahl was right! There was a connection between the Egyptian and American civilizations. Are you familiar at all with the story of the Danish King, Dan I

"I can't say that I am," Larkin replied, "but I'm sure it's fascinating." Larkin was amazed at how much information his young colleague had amassed. He seemed to soak up knowledge like a sponge.

"There is evidence that King Priam of Troy was a direct descendant of Judah through Judah's grandson, Dara (Dardanus,

King of Dardania), who died in 1414 BC. Of course, Judah was a direct descendant of Adam, as you probably know."

"I do seem to recall that from my study of the Old Testament," said Larkin, "But that was a few years ago." Larkin was beginning to feel that attending church was something he should take up again.

"Well," said Hector, "Bare with me as I try to explain this. The eighth king in descent from Priam was Seskef ("the Sheaf"). Seskef went by several names. To the Norwegians he was called Votan or Odin II (Odin I being none other than Nimrod, who built the Tower of Babel.). To the Danes he was known as Danus or Dan I. This is how the story goes:

"Denmark originally received its name from the ancient Tribe of Danaan. It would pass to the king who took the name of the subjects over whom he ruled. In 1040 BC, there was a break-up in the German state, when the three sons of the German King Wolfheim—Kells, Gall and Hiller—left the seafarers of northwest Europe without a leader. So, the German and Hebrew inhabitants of Denmark decided to select a scion of the royal Trojan house to reign over them. That scion was Seskef, who took the name Danus or Dan I. At the time of his selection he was living in Thrace, which would be northern Greece and southern Bulgaria today. Dan answered the call and led a large migration out of Thrace into Denmark. He reigned as King of Denmark from 1040 BC until 999 BC, and it was while he was king that his story becomes even more fantastic. Soon after establishing his new kingdom in Denmark, Dan set out on a trip across the seas to establish a new colony.

"I have studied all the ancient writings," Hector said, "and among those is the *Popul Vuh*, an ancient writing of the Quiche Maya people, who lived beside the Usumacinta River in ancient Mexico. These writings clearly indicate that the ancient Maya traveled westward across the Atlantic Ocean to Mexico!"

"What?" Larkin said. "That flies directly in the face of traditional thinking. Are you sure?"

"I'm positive," said Hector. "And who was the 'great ruler' who led the Quiche Maya to their new home in Mexico? The Maya claimed that their kingdom was founded by a ruler named Votan, Oden or Dan. He was a white man, who came by sea from the east around 1,000 BC. Scandinavian literature is filled with accounts of Dan's distant journeys, which took him away from his homeland for many months, sometimes even years."

"Look," said Larkin, "All this may be true, but if, as you say, this Dan did come west, he couldn't have come alone? Who came with him?"

"Red men," said Hector, half jokingly. "You see, Jonas, in ancient times, the people of Thrace were descendants of Tiras, son of Japheth (Old Testament, Genesis, Chapter 10, verse 2). You really need to catch up on your Bible reading."

"I've been meaning to do just that," Larkin retorted, half sincerely.

"Yes, well, the ancient Thraceans were known as 'red men', because of their fierce appearance, their swarthy skin, and their often tattooed and painted bodies. When Dan migrated to Denmark many of these 'red men' came with him. And, when he journeyed to America, they accompanied him there as well."

"So the Mayan culture owes its creation to a Danish king who sailed across the Atlantic Ocean to Mexico with a bunch of red men from the north of Greece. Does that pretty much sum it up?" asked Larkin.

"You've condensed it a little more than I would have, but, yes, that sums it up."

"I think I'm ready for another drink. Do you need a refill?"

"Yes, thank you."

Larkin poured two more scotches. Hector was on a roll.

"Anyway, after years of researching the old records, and plotting the observations which were recorded, I am convinced that the Earth was visited by extraterrestrial beings as far back as 12,000 BC, and that they continued to make periodic return visits until about 1,500 BC. They were the gods of Mt. Olympus. They were the gods of ancient Egypt. They were the gods of the Sumerians, the Ethiopians, the ancient Chinese, as well as the Aztecs. I'm sure of it."

"What about the God of Abraham and Ishmael?" Larkin added.

"Actually, Genesis fits in very well with my theory," Hector replied. "Did you know that if one adds up all the generations between Adam and, let's say, Jacob, as described in Genesis, one obtains a total of 9,297 years. Of course, I don't believe that these generations were single individuals. Adam could not possibly have lived 930 years. No. Each of these generations probably was a *clan*, or a tribe of people sharing a common name. But, be that as it may, the total from Adam to Jacob is 9,297 years. Now, since Dara, Judah's grandson, died in 1414 BC, it's likely that Judah lived at about 1500 BC. Judah, of course, was a son of Jacob. So, by adding 9,297 to 1,500, one obtains a total of 10,797 years, or rounded to11,000 BC as the time when Adam probably walked the Earth."

"So," said Larkin, "Your alien visitors may have known Adam."

"They not only knew him," Hector said. "I think they created him!"

"Created him, eh?" Larkin asked, as he re-lit his pipe.

"Don't tell me you're actually beginning to believe my story," Hector asked, somewhat amused.

"A scientist must approach everything with an open mind," Larkin responded, "no matter how fantastic it sounds. Well, Hec, you've told me all about the 'when'. I guess the next question has to be 'where?' Where did they come from?"

They both sat down at Larkin's desk. Hector took a pencil and began drawing on a legal pad. "This is the constellation Orion," he said as he drew a diagram of the hunter. "Remember, I told you that the pyramids of Egypt were arranged in the same configuration as Orion's belt."

"Yes," said Larkin.

"And here, to the southwest of Orion is Canis Major," Hector said, as he drew the diagram of Orion's hunting dog.

"OK," said Larkin.

"Now," said Hector, "if I draw a line through the belt of Orion and continue to the southwest, the line points directly to this big star at the top of Canis Major."

"I see," said Larkin. "What's that big star called?"

"That, my friend, is Sirius," said Hector. "Sirius, also known as the Dog Star. The brightest star in the heavens." He then began to rattle off facts, as if astronomy were second nature to him. "Although the brightest, Sirius is only 1.5 Sun diameters. Its brightness comes from the fact that it is only 8.56 light years away, making it the sixth closest star. The star is a binary, but its companion is very dim and very close. The companion is a white dwarf, which wasn't confirmed until 1862. Named Sirius B or The Pup, it's an eighth magnitude star with an estimated radius of only ten thousand kilometers, about twice the size of Earth. Yet its mass is nearly equal to that of our Sun's, which means that a teaspoon full of The Pup would weigh over a ton!"

"And Sirius is where your aliens came from?" asked Larkin.

"Let me explain," said Hector. "Sirius was a very important star in ancient times. For example, the Athenian New Year began with the appearance of Sirius. He was seen as two-headed, like the Roman God Janus: looking back at the past year and forward to the new one. Rather ironic since the ancient Greeks couldn't possibly have known that Sirius was binary. The Sumerians based all their gods on stars, and Ninurta, or Sirius, was worshipped as the judge of the universe, who passed sentence on mankind. The Egyptians based their calendar on the heliacal risings of Sirius, even though, in Egypt, Sirius can only be seen in the early dawn, just above the horizon. Why didn't the Egyptians use the Sun and Moon relationship, instead of a star they could barely see? Sirius was also worshipped as the bringer of the annual Nile floods, and 'creator of all green growing things'."

"This is all well and good" Larkin interrupted, "but you haven't indicated that any planets orbit Sirius. How could there be any life there?"

"Sirius isn't necessarily the home of these aliens. I believe it serves as a beacon. Not only is it close and very bright, but the fact that it's binary adds to it. Alpha and Beta Sirius orbit each other once every 50.09 years, at a distance comparable to Uranus orbiting the Sun. The gravitational forces of such an arrangement give Sirius a very erratic course when seen through a telescope. Consequently, Sirius has attracted a great deal of attention from astronomers over the years—precisely what the aliens wanted. There's one more interesting feature, Jonas."

"And that is?" Larkin asked, as he looked at Hector's drawings again.

"Although Sirius is not very prominent in the Northern Hemisphere, it is a dominant feature in the Southern Hemisphere, particularly during the winter solstice in June. Also, we know that Stonehenge in England was built for Sun worship, but the stones are arranged in such a way as to place specific interest on the Sun's reflections at the winter and spring solstices. Finally, Jonas, there's this. According to Inca legend, the god of creation, Viracocha created the Earth and the heavens from darkness. He fashioned men from clay and breathed life into them. He placed them in Tihuanaco (their 'Garden of Eden'), taught them language, customs and arts. He punished them with a great flood, and then, *flew* some of them to other continents so that they could spread all over the Earth. Does this sound familiar?"

"Certainly," Larkin replied. "It sounds like Genesis."

"Exactly, Jonas. My research tells me that the belief in a Sun god, which occurred in later cultures, was directly linked to belief in Sirius. And, Jonas, my finding of the Egyptian scroll in the Amazon, telling the biblical story of the great flood, is further evidence that all of these cultures have a common denominator.

"But you can't deny that all this is still pure speculation," argued Larkin, "There still isn't any proof!"

"Very well, Jonas," Hector sighed, "believe what you will. As for me, I know that Ninurta, Viracocha, Zeus, and even Jehovah, were one in the same—Aliens. Aliens who came here, and worked their 'miracles'. Aliens who made us what we are, and who left us with a sign. A beacon in the heavens for all of us to see—perhaps a warning button for us to push—Sirius."

"Well," said Larkin, as he stood up to stretch his legs. It was quite late, but he still had questions. "I guess that leaves 'how?' Speaking of which, how about one more for the road?"

"No, thanks," Hector replied, "I thought I'd already told you that."

"Most of what you've been telling me all evening is 'Why'. Now I want to know exactly how you plan to do this transmission."

"The transmission will originate from the observatory at Huancayo," Hector reiterated. "As I've already said, mathematical equations are the one language they're certain to understand. By using a laser beam as a visual sign, in conjunction with a radio transmission signal of the message, we should be able to establish contact."

"That's a mighty big 'if'," Larkin injected. "You're talking about a very small target, 8.56 light years away, and even if you get that far, there's no guarantee that anyone will be there to receive the message. It's all speculation still. Besides, at the speed of light, we're talking a minimum of, let's see, 17.12 years for he message to get there, to be received, and to have the answer transmitted back here—if there *is* an answer—which I doubt."

"I agree that it's a tremendous risk. Even crazy, perhaps. But all the evidence I've collected over the past ten years points to Sirius, and if, after hearing me out, you want to back out of it, that's fine. I'll take the computer and go back alone," Hector said in a tone of half anger, half disappointment.

"All right, Hec," Larkin said, visibly amused. He'd had Hector going there for a minute. "I know you're a great scientist, and you obviously believe in what you're doing. A scientist always pursues things to their logical conclusion, and if this is the conclusion you've drawn, you must pursue it. You need my computer, and things will go a lot smoother if I'm there to run it. I can't say I'm in complete agreement with you, but that doesn't mean you're wrong. I'm still in. By the way, when do you plan to make the transmission?"

Hector smiled, "At the beginning of the winter solstice in the Southern Hemisphere. Midnight on June 19, next year, and I plan a transmission lasting twenty-four hours."

"So," Larkin calculated. "We send the message June 19, 2002, twenty-four hours in length, ending at midnight on June 20. That means, if all goes well...."

Hector interrupted, "We should have an answer on, or after, July 29, 2019."

"You're sure?" Larkin asked, knowing Hector couldn't be wrong.

"Yes, anytime after 7:55 p.m."

"I see," said Larkin, "and what frequency do you plan to use?" Obviously, Hector had been planning for this moment for years.

"Believe it or not," Hector said, "that decision was easy. Daniken and others have suggested 1420 megahertz, and their logic is excellent. This frequency is outside those used on Earth, and it is the same as the radiation frequency of neutral hydrogen, caused by the collision of hydrogen atoms. Since hydrogen is the first, and most basic of the elemental structures, its properties must be known throughout the universe. If anyone is there, they should receive us."

"Well, I guess you've about covered everything, for now anyway," Larkin said, as he stood. He was stiff, and it was nearly three in the morning. They'd been at it for eleven hours, and Hector still didn't look tired. The man's stamina was amazing.

All that remained now was to get the equipment to Peru, install it, compute and re-compute, send the message, and sit back and wait—for a little over seventeen years! No problem.

"I guess we'd better break this up for tonight," Larkin said. "I'll start the wheels rolling tomorrow. We'll ship everything by air. It'll save time."

"Excellent," Hector said, "There's an airfield at Pucallpa, but I hope you're not planning on using a 747."

"No. We'll use smaller planes, and make several trips, if necessary, from Lima."

"Good," Hector said, somewhat relieved, "We can truck it from there. My complex is only about ten miles away, on the Ucayali River. I can get boats, too."

"How about assistants?" Larkin asked.

"Don't worry," Hector laughed, "the entire Archaeology Department of the University of Lima is there, and I've got as many graduate students as we need. In Peru, Jonas, there is never a labor shortage."

"OK then," Larkin said, "I guess we're ready to start. When are you going back?"

"Tomorrow—er—today," Hector replied, "I've got to begin planning immediately. June 19th is only a year away, and we have to be ready then, or its another year's delay."

"Here we are worrying about a year," Larkin said, "and our visitors were here 12,000 years ago. That's a long time in human history."

"Yes, it seems that way to us; but, what is 12,000 years to a god? A week, a month—or a minute. How long does it take for bacteria to overrun a petri dish? Time is a relative thing. I don't think 12,000 years is long at all in the whole scheme of things."

"I suppose that's true, Larkin added, "after all, the Earth is four or five billion years old. To it, mankind probably seems like a twenty-four hour bug."

CHAPTER IV

SPRING VALLEY

The two men walked out of Larkin's office. The corridors were darkened, and only the security guards were present. The underground parking garage resembled a tomb, as they stepped up to Jonas' car. The only one left, except for those belonging to the guards. Jonas loved this old car, a 1987 Mercedes Benz 560 SL convertible coupe. Navy blue, because Jonas had been in the Navy. Fourteen years old, but she could still move.

"Do you mind if I put the top down?" he asked Hector.

"I'd love it," Hector responded. Together they lowered the top into its compartment in the rear—no automatic top on this old girl.

Jonas pulled out of the garage, and headed for the Waldorf, where Hector was staying. They didn't say anything during the drive. Hector took in the sights and Jonas just thought about what had transpired during the evening. Perhaps enough had been said already. As the Mercedes eased up to the entrance, and the doorman approached, Hector turned to Jonas, and said, "Thank you for showing me the computer, Jonas. Think about what we've discussed tonight, and let me know what your arrangements are as soon as possible."

"I will, Hec," Jonas replied, as Hector stepped out of the car. "Good night."

"Good night to you, as well, my friend," Hector replied.

After dropping Hector off, Jonas headed uptown, across the George Washington Bridge and drove home to Spring Valley. It was a cool summer night, and being in a short-sleeved shirt made it a bit uncomfortable but Jonas didn't mind, and the cold wind blowing through the open car kept him awake.

Upon arriving home, he pulled into the driveway, pushing the garage door button as he did so. Stopping short of the open garage, he turned off the engine and sat in the silence of the moment. He had warned Patty that morning that it would be a long day, and after twenty-seven years of marriage she knew what that meant—another all-nighter at the office. The night was clear, at least clear by New York standards, and as he looked up to the sky he could see a few stars. As he watched them twinkle he couldn't help but wonder.

Was it logical, or even reasonable, to assume that in all the vastness of space, Earth was the only living planet? His mind drifted back to a lecture he'd heard years ago, or was it an article he'd read? No matter. The Milky Way, he remembered, was one of twenty galaxies within a radius of 1.5 million light years of Earth. Telescopes, he'd been told back then, could detect one hundred million trillion stars within just the vicinity of Earth. Of those stars, how many had planets? One in a thousand, perhaps? That's one hundred million billion. Of those, how many had planets which could support life? Another one in a thousand? That's one hundred trillion. And of those, how many actually did support life? One in a thousand, again. Now we were down to a mere one hundred billion. And of these, how many contained intelligent life? One in a thousand. That's one hundred million planets containing intelligent life. And, of this number, how many contain life as intelligent, or more intelligent, than Mankind? One in a thousand? Now we were down to one hundred thousand possible planets, which are like Earth! Who was to say that one of these planets, at some remote time in the past, didn't develop slightly more rapidly than Earth; didn't discover space travel before we did. What's a few thousand years in the vastness of space—a second—a minute? Who really knew?

Jonas kept staring at the stars, It was now nearing five a.m., and the Sun was starting to rise. The first birds were chirping, and a new day was beginning.

Jonas turned on the engine, pulled the car into the garage, turned off the engine again and closed the door behind him. Getting out, he grabbed his briefcase containing the night's work, and headed into the house.

The Larkin residence was a large Tudor-style, located on a quiet cul-de-sac in an exclusive development known as Quail Hollow. It abutted the Quail Hollow Country Club, where the Larkins were members, but Jonas rarely found time to play. The house was tastefully decorated in Victorian era furnishings, all selected by Patty Larkin herself. Although Victorian in appearance, the house boasted nearly every technological marvel known to man, from its state-of-the-art security system to the latest audio and video equipment in the media room The landscaping was formal, complete with mandatory fountain and waterfall. The tennis court and swimming pool had been installed years ago and were still meticulously maintained.

By far Jonas' favorite room in the house had to be the recreation room in the basement. It reflected both his and Patty's favorite interests and fondest memories.

Patty was a whiz at jigsaw puzzles. In a single evening she could complete a 500-piece puzzle. These usually measured approximately twenty-four by eighteen inches. Other puzzles varied in size from very small to very large. One puzzle, measuring only two inches by two inches, contained a hundred pieces, which had to be assembled using tweezers. Other puzzles were giants, measuring four feet by three feet, with two thousand pieces. Those had to be assembled on tables. Once completed, it would be Jonas' job to preserve each puzzle so that it wouldn't come apart. This was accomplished by brushing a layer of white Mod Podge® on top of the completed puzzle. When dry, the substance became transparent and turned the puzzle into a solid sheet. Over the years Patty had completed nearly a thousand puzzles, containing nearly a half million pieces! Jonas had counted them.

While Patty was engaged in this activity, Jonas had been busy, collecting old record albums. With the advent of compact discs in the 1980's, vinyl record albums had become obsolete. However, their record jackets, being slightly larger than one square foot, were colorful and informative. Many of the older ones were not re-issued in compact disc format, and were therefore quite valuable. Jonas also collected old 78 rpm records, specializing in John McCormack and Paul Whiteman. Jonas had hundreds of albums, hundreds of 45 rpm records, and hundreds of 78's. They reminded him of his boyhood back in Cleveland, where as a young boy, he remembered when he first heard the jukebox in Mac's Café.

The Glenville area of Cleveland was bustling in the late 1950's. Jonas, his parents and his two younger sisters lived in an apartment on the corner of East 102nd Street and St. Clair Avenue.

This was no ordinary apartment. Formerly the residence of a physician, it boasted twelve-foot ceilings, a study with sliding doors, a pantry with a potato bin, and maid's quarters in the back. That's where Jonas' oldest sister, Ruthie, slept. There were three gigantic bay windows, and the corner one had a conical roof with a weather vane perched on top. The bathroom featured an enormous bathtub with claw legs, and a pedestal sink, both with gleaming brass fixtures. There was even a skylight. The rooms were huge. The dining room alone measured twenty-five feet across. The family used it as a combination living/dining area. In addition to these amenities, the apartment also featured foot-long rats, and a boiler that broke down every January. Jonas' mother and father slept in the study and his younger sister, Alice, joined them there after her arrival in 1957. This meant that Jonas got to sleep in the parlor. The parlor contained that wonderful corner bay window, which allowed him to see all the way down the street. There was also a smaller leaded glass window to the right, which produced "rainbows" when he tilted his head a certain way. Sleeping in the parlor also meant that Jonas was directly above Mac's Café.

Mac's Café had formerly been a drug store. It boasted the tall ceiling of molded tin, with fans whirring to distribute the cigarette smoke evenly throughout. It had a tile floor, and a bar, which extended the entire length. There were bar stools, and booths along the outer wall by the side street. The back bar was ornately carved and all the liquor bottles were lined up in rows in front of the mirror like soldiers for dress inspection. The main entrance was on the corner, below Jonas' bay window, and to the right of the entrance, in front of the window with the flashing Budweiser Beer sign, stood the jukebox.

At first, she'd been a Wurlitzer®, standing there like a small temple in her majestic splendor. The lights of red, blue, green and yellow would change magically as the oil bubbles moved up the sides. Jonas watched in awe as a customer dropped a nickel in the slot and pushed a button. The machine seemed to come to life. The records (78's, of course) were stored horizontally, each in its own little *house*. The *house*, which corresponded with the number on the button would smoothly swing out. Then, the turntable would start turning and rise up, lift the record from its holder and continue up until it reached the tone arm, which seemed to always *know* where the start of the record was. Music would then come out of the speaker on the bottom.

Later, Jonas remembered, perhaps around 1957, they hauled out the old Wurlitzer®, and replaced it with a Seeberg Select-O-Matic®. This machine played the newer 45's which were stored perpendicularly along the back of the machine. The *player*, which consisted of the tone arm and turntable, also perpendicular, would glide alond a track in front of the record rack. The customer would drop a dime or quarter in the slot, and push a button. The *player* would move along the track until it positioned itself in front of the record selected. Then, magically, the record would pop out of its slot, into the player, the turntable would whirl, and the tone arm would swing over and catch the groove on the record. Fascinating. Jonas could (and did) watch it for hours.

Both these jukeboxes stood in the same spot, directly beneath Jonas' bed in the parlor upstairs. And, every night he would be serenaded to sleep, or kept awake, by the wonderful sounds they produced. Perry Como would fill the room with his voice, or maybe it would be the Platters, or Tony Bennett, Billy Vaughn, or the McGuire Sisters. Frankie Yankovic might follow with "Just Because." One night Jonas counted Tennessee Ernie Ford singing "Sixteen Tons" sixteen times.

Those were great times, which was why Jonas and Patty decided that their recreation room would be unique. The walls were papered with Patty's jigsaw puzzles, and the ceiling was covered with album covers. Naturally, a Seeberg jukebox, filled with 45's adorned one wall, and there were numerous photographs of entertainers from the 50's and 60's, many of them autographed. There were two pinball machines, one of which, entitled "Funhouse" Patty and Jonas used to play at Geneva-on-the-Lake, Ohio, years ago. Jonas admired Pat Lawlor's work. The so-called "Father of Pinball Machines," Lawlor, who was responsible for the design of many of the most popular machines of the late twentieth century. Many considered "Funhouse," featuring Rudy's talking head, to be his finest achievement. Jonas loved the inner workings of these machines, and loved to tinker with them.

The Larkin children, Holly and Matthew, who also enjoyed those things as children were now grown. Holly, a graduate student at Columbia, was following in her father's footsteps, and studying computer science. Matthew, who was two years younger, had just graduated from Kent State University, Jonas' undergraduate alma mater, with a major in journalism.

Although full-grown adults now, Matthew would always be "Matty" to his Dad, and Holly would always be "Punkin". She earned that nickname on her first Halloween. Was it really that long ago when Holly was a six-ear old girl, with curly blond hair and dimples?

Jonas recalled how very impatient Holly was about that Halloween that year. She started nagging Mommy and Daddy two weeks early about getting a "punkin", as she called it. Her friend, Johnny, who lived five doors away, had a whole garage full of pumpkins for sale, and she could hardly wait to buy one. She was very persistent and persuasive because Daddy gave in after only a few days. Jonas could still remember the look on her face as he handed her the dollar to buy her pumpkin.

She told Daddy that she already had her "punkin" picked out. It was round and beautiful and it sat on the edge of the top shelf of Johnny's garage. Holly grabbed the handle of her shiny, new red wagon and walked majestically to Johnny's house with Matty tagging close behind. Like most younger brothers, Matty later told about what happened next.

Holly pulled the wagon up to the garage. The door was open and she could see her pumpkin sitting on the shelf. She ran to Johnny's back door and knocked. No one answered. She knocked again, but their car was gone so she guessed they weren't home. A combined feeling of despair and anger must have swept over her, but it was quickly dispelled by a brilliant idea. Leaving the money under a rock on the back porch, she pulled the wagon inside the garage and positioned it just below the shelf where her pumpkin was. She and Matty found a crate and placed it in the wagon so that when she stood on it she could reach her prize.

Balancing herself on top of the crate, Holly could barely reach it, so she called down to her brother, "I'm gonna throw it down, and when it stops bouncin' we'll pick it up and put it in the wagon."

Holly eased her pumpkin over the edge, and like a meteorite colliding with earth, her pumpkin hit the ground and exploded all over the garage. Holly stood there on top of the crate, in utter shock. Her mouth was agape. Matty started to cry. Panic reigned. Holly quickly reached for another pumpkin, grabbed it, held on to it for dear life, climbed down to the floor, threw off the crate, set the pumpkin in the wagon, ran home with wagon in tow, and then ran straight to her room. Patty guessed something was wrong because the pumpkin in the wagon was downright ugly, certainly not the one Holly had been bragging about.

When Johnny and his parents got home, they saw the mess, found the money, put two and two together, and called Patty. The punishment was just. Holly paid for the second pumpkin with money from her piggy bank, and Mom used the broken pumpkin to show Holly how pies were made.

For the next few days the weather was warm. Mom had stored the second pumpkin in the back pantry, and Holly could hardly wait for Daddy to carve it. The day before Halloween Jonas reached in the cupboard to get it. All he got was the stem! If Holly thought the mess in the garage was bad, this one was much worse. There was green, rotting, smelly pumpkin all over the cupboard.

To top things off, it snowed on Halloween night, and the kids couldn't go out.

All that was left were the pies from the broken pumpkin, and Jonas could still recall how those were the best "punkin" pies he'd ever had.

47

And that was how Holly became "Punkin."

They were both good kids, Jonas knew, but most of the credit belonged to his long suffering wife, who put up with his crazy work schedule all these years, and still managed to keep their family together.

Patty, a second grade schoolteacher by profession, and two years his junior, had met Jonas on a blind date twenty-eight years ago, and it had been love at first sight, although their engagement was nearly a year. She had stood by him through good times and bad. She had taught school while her husband worked on his undergraduate, masters and doctorate, and he had stood by her through health problems. Patty was a borderline diabetic, and her second pregnancy had been especially difficult. The doctors recommended abortion, but Patty and Jonas decided to see it through. Matthew confirmed their decision everyday.

Jonas opened the kitchen door, pressed the code on the security system touch pad, and walked in. Setting his briefcase down on the counter he walked over to the refrigerator, opened it, and started staring at the contents.

"'That's the trouble with those things. You gotta watch them all the time.'" his lovely wife quoted from their favorite film, *The Big Chill*, as she came in the room. He turned toward Patty. They embraced as if they hadn't seen each other for a week. Actually, it *had* been nearly a week. Ever since Jonas had started working on the 770, their time together had been minimal. Jonas caressed and kissed his brown-haired beauty with her green eyes. "Another long one, eh?" she said, as he held her close. "I was beginning to think you wouldn't make it home at all."

"I very nearly didn't," Jonas said. "I met the most incredible person today, honey, that I've ever seen. A true genius, who thinks we've been visited by aliens."

"I see," said Patty, "and where were you all day? At the hospital?" she joked, as she started to make coffee.

48

"No, honey, we were at the office. He wants to use my computer to contact them."

"Uh-huh," she said, as she started pouring water in the coffee maker. "How about some bacon and eggs? You sound like your brain needs some food in it."

"Sure," Jonas said as he sat down at the counter. "His name is Hector Rimirez Villa-Ramos, and he's a twenty-something Ph.D. from M.I.T. and Peru. He wants to send signals to Sirius—you know—the Dog Star—and wait nineteen years for an answer." Jonas was clearly running out of gas. He was exhausted.

"And are you going to help him?" Patty asked, as she walked over to the refrigerator, and started removing eggs, bread, butter and bacon.

"Yeah—I want to," Jonas hesitated, "but there's a problem...."

"You mean other than the fact that the guy sounds like a nut case?" Patty asked.

"No. He's not a nut case. I think he may be on to something."

"Or on something," she added, jokingly. "What's this other problem?"

"The problem, honey, is—he wants me to come with him—I mean, I *want* to go with him—to Peru—to work with him."

"Peru," Patty stopped short. "How long?"

"A year."

"A year."

"Maybe a little longer if there are problems."

Patty resumed making breakfast, not saying anything. Larkin could hear the coffee maker start perking. Patty beat the eggs, started frying the bacon and put the bread in the toaster. She put the beaten eggs in another greased pan, and took out two plates and two cups from the cupboard. Jonas got the utensils from the drawer and set them on the counter. When finished, Patty served the food, while Jonas poured the coffee. Not a word was spoken. They sat down and started to eat.

"When do you have to be there?" Patty asked, as she looked at her husband.

Jonas looked up at his wife's face. After twenty-eight years they knew each other. They each knew that he had to do this. "Hector's leaving today. I should follow him as soon as possible, I guess."

"Next week?"

"Next week.

They resumed eating. They finished, cleaned up the kitchen, and went upstairs to the master suite. Patty wasn't talking, and Jonas was even more tired. The coffee had had little effect.

Patty had climbed back into bed, and after Jonas undressed he climbed in beside her. They both lay there staring at the ceiling. Neither could sleep. "Who'd have thought," Patty finally said, "that two young college people living on Hamburger Helper® back in the 70's would be living the good life here in Spring Valley today."

"Yeah," Jonas said, "we've come a long way, honey."

"Remember that house we were living in while you were finishing your senior year at Kent?" Patty asked. "330 North Willow."

"I'll never forget it," Jonas laughed. "You could always tell when someone was banging away upstairs because the dining room light would shake.

"And remember when you were working as a stock boy at Penney's® to help pay the bills?" Patty laughed.

"God, yes," Jonas replied. "I'll never forget dropping that pool table in the parking lot, and then picking it up and putting it in the wrong truck."

"No wonder that guy didn't complain before he drove off," Patty laughed.

"Yeah," Jonas said, as he began re-living those days. "Working for pennies at Penney's®" Jonas called it in an article he wrote for the Kent State University Yearbook, the Chestnut Burr:

"I decided when I graduated from high school that I would go to college so I wouldn't have to push heavy crates around in a warehouse for the rest of my life. However, I soon found myself pushing heavy crates around in a warehouse trying to earn enough money to go to college so that when I graduated I probably would end up working in a warehouse teaching other college students how to push heavy crates around.

"It was 1974 and I was earning about a dollar above the minimum wage, which was also about a dollar below the cost of living. In addition, I received a fifteen-percent discount on any item purchased in the store. The management thought this was a great benefit, but they knew that on my salary I'd never be able to afford anything anyway.

"Welcome to the Penney's® stockroom. The moment they hired me they gave me a nametag and a piece of tape with my name embossed on it from one of those lettering guns. I stuck the tape on the tag and wore it whenever I was working so they would know whom to blame. This tag was very useful. It threatened me with tetanus whenever I stuck it in my chest; it got tangled in every package I picked up; and, it cost twenty-five cents to replace if I lost it.

"Working in the stockroom was anything but dull. One day I'd be stacking a shipment of ice boxes on top hat boxes (because 'I' follows 'H'), and the next day I'd be taking a cart full of oven cleaner to the Beauty Aids Department (I guess this was for ladies who wanted to wipe their faces off completely.).

"I shall now attempt to describe the delicate art of stacking crates. Like any profession, stocking has its own jargon. Forget such flowery phrases as 'fragile—handle with care,' or 'do not stack more than three boxes high,' or better yet, 'store in a cool, dry place.' The only ones required are 'kick', 'jab', 'toss' (if it's light), 'throw' (if it's heavy), 'stick by the heater' (if it's chocolate), and 'put on top of Italian crystal' (if it's a freezer). In addition

51

to phrases, stocking also has a unique numbering system. Each crate has a collection of numbers longer than the crate itself. First, there's the order number (for example, a radio may be ordered as ZK96732); then the crate number, if there is more than one crate in the shipment (crate no. 2); then there's the lot number (4077); a sub-division (364); a style number (47); a color code (R4, for red); a department number (2A, second floor, appliance); and the price ($24.95 each). Let's assume that I'm in the stockroom and the phone rings. 'Hello, stockroom,' I say as I answer it. A voice on the other end says, 'I want a ZK96732-2-4077-364-47-R4-2A-$24.95 immediately,' and then hangs up. In the meantime I'm trying to find a pencil and paper so I can take down the message. If I had gotten the numbers I would be expected to know what it was, where it was, where it's going, and how to get it there in less than five minutes. The Olympic Committee ought to consider this—a gold medal for stock searching.

"Every stock boy has his favorite item. One that he will never forget, probably because of the pain it produced. About two weeks before Thanksgiving, the Sporting Goods Department decided that a 'hot' item for the Christmas season would be sets of barbells. I'll never forget that day. One hundred sets of one hundred-pound weights arrived with one hundred ten-pound bars to go with them. Oh joy! Oh rupture! There we were, the whole crew, carrying boxes of weights off the truck and stacking them in the freight elevator, for the trip upstairs to the stockroom. (Why the architect who designed this store decided to put the stockroom on the second floor instead of on the ground floor will forever remain a mystery.). In any event, we finally got them loaded onto the elevator, and pushed the button.

"Only after the sounds of snapping cables, grinding gears and blown motors had ceased, and only after the smell of burning electrical wires and ozone had started to fade, did someone bother to check the weight limit on the freight elevator. In our eagerness to get the weights up to the stockroom, we somehow managed to put 11,100 pounds of barbells in an elevator designed to hold only 5,000. So, now, of course, we were forced to carry the barbells upstairs by hand. Oh rupture!

"Once we got them upstairs, we had a new problem. If we stacked all the barbells in one place, the weight could cause the floor to cave in, which would have a decidedly negative impact on the innocent customers who were shopping underneath. So, we divided the barbells into five stacks of twenty sets each, and spread them around the stockroom. By the time Christmas Eve arrived only about half had been sold, and the rest had to be carried down to the loading dock for return. Oh rupture! "The phone rings again. It's the appliance manager. 'Where's that radio we ordered?' 'Could you please repeat the number?' I ask sheepishly. 'Yes, it's ZK96732-2-4077-364-47-R4-2A-$24.95, and hurry up! The customer's waiting.'

"Penney's® carries many models of radios and they are all stored on the top shelf of the rear rack of the rear half of the rear stockroom between stuffed rabbits and raincoats. And so the safari begins—through aprons, bananas, china and doors, electric blankets, linoleum floors, go-carts and high-chairs and good Irish stew, jewelry, kimonos and licorice, too; mittens and napkins and ogres that roar; yellow wax pears that don't have a core; quilts, rabbits and radios—radios! At last, there they are, but first I must go over to S's and borrow a stepladder. Unfortunately, since there are none in stock, I'll have to use P.E.P., the Penney Emergency Plan.

"I hate using P.E.P. because it's so dangerous. The first time I attempted it I placed my left foot on the first shelf of the left rack, and my right foot on the first shelf of the right rack. Then, I moved my left foot up to the second shelf, and my right foot up to the second. By repeating the process I should have reached the top eventually, but I never did. While climbing up the shelves my right shoe became untied, and by the third shelf, which was seven feet from the floor, the shoe was ready to fall off. At this moment, I heard a ripping sound and felt a draft between my legs. There I stood, like the Colossus of Rhodes awaiting the earthquake, with my pants torn and my right foot on very shaky ground. Had not another stock boy come to my rescue I might not have lived to tell this tale, which probably won't gladden the hearts of too many readers.

"Anyway, this time I manage to get up there. Of course, the box numbers are facing the wall, so I have to turn them all around to find the right one. Then, I have to lower the box and myself one shelf at a time until I reach the floor. I run out to the department, and hand the box to the sales clerk, only to find that the customer has just left, muttering angry words about poor service.

"I return to the stockroom feeling overjoyed. Work will be a little easier from now on. The J.C. Penney Company® has just lost another customer.

Jonas and Patty laughed every time they remembered that story. "I can't imagine why they fired such a good worker," Patty said, laughing.

"Neither can I," Jonas laughed as well. "It's a good thing I knew something about mathematics and physics, or we'd still be on welfare. Do you remember that first calculator you bought me from Radio Shack®, honey?"

"I'll never forget it. It cost me $89.95, and they wouldn't let you use it in physics class. They said it gave you an 'unfair advantage,' and they made you use a slide rule on all your exams."

"Yeah, and I've still got that old calculator on display in my office," Jonas said. "If it were any older the display would show Roman numerals." They both laughed, as they lay in bed, thinking about the past.

"We had some good times back then," Patty said. "Remember when you were a member of the V.F.W. in Kent, and you worked there as a bartender?"

"God, yes," Jonas replied. "That's when I was President of the Kent State Veterans Association. Remember that homecoming game, when we brought the vets down from the V.A. Hospital in Cleveland?"

"How could I forget it?" Patty said. "I was helping the Ladies Auxiliary in the kitchen, remember?"

"Oh, yes, the corned beef and cabbage," Jonas recalled, and with that his mind drifted back to that November day in 1974.

It was a cold, snowy Saturday at the Kent State University Homecoming. The Kent Golden Flashes were going to play Utah that afternoon. Early that morning a bunch of KSU students drove up to Cleveland and helped bring some disabled veterans from the V.A. Hospital to see the game. First they were treated to dinner at the old Kentwood Restaurant. About seventy seats had been reserved for them, as well as for handicapped KSU students, their volunteer helpers, and members of the KSU Vets Association. Jonas remembered that about ninety people showed up. "How was that for student apathy?" he asked Patty.

"Not bad," she answered.

"After dinner we went to the game," Jonas continued. "We had great seats—end zone on the Utah side. Of course, wheelchairs couldn't go up into the stands, so we couldn't get any closer to the game. We sat there, huddled in blankets, shouting cheers and gazing at the acres of empty seats around us. By the third quarter it was bitterly cold out there. When you can't stand up to cheer, or walk around, your limbs become frozen, but those people hung in there as long as they could, cheering the Flashes on."

"I remember this one vet," Jonas said, his voice nearly breaking. "He was a black paraplegic, whose wife came along with him. They brought a bottle along in order to keep warm. Although he tried to hide it, he was shivering so bad you could hear his teeth chattering. Finally, even though a cop was watching us, I reached into his bag, pulled out that bottle, unscrewed the cap, held it to his mouth and tilted it. The cop never said a word."

"Midway through the fourth quarter the snow was blowing so hard we couldn't see. The disabled vets and students were frozen. We helped load them back onto their bus. Half of us rode along with them to the V.F.W. post in town, while the rest stayed on for the final gun. We yelled and cheered for our team—but nobody heard us," Jonas added.

"What was the final score?" Patty asked.

"Isn't that strange," Jonas reflected, "I can remember the color of that guy's hat (It was green.), even the booze he was drinking (It was Canadian Club®.), but for the life of me I can't remember the score. I guess it wasn't important."

"Anyway," Jonas continued, after a short pause, "when we got to the V.F.W. each wheelchair had to be carried up thirteen steps to the second floor (Isn't it funny how I can remember that, but I can't remember the score.). Those chairs were battery-operated, and they weighed a ton. It took four guys to carry each one up, and there were a dozen chairs.

"I'll never forget that fantastic spread you and the other women in the Ladies Auxiliary prepared for us, honey," Jonas smiled as he looked over to his wife.

"I won't forget it, either, dear. While you and the other guys were at the game we were busy in the kitchen all afternoon, peeling potatoes, cutting cabbage, simmering the corned beef...."

"Well," Jonas interrupted, "at least you were warm."

"That's true," Patty said, "and the girl talk and companionship was great. Remember how we had to help feed some of those people?"

"Remember?" Jonas said. "One of the wheelchairs had a student who was majoring in business administration. I'll never forget him. You had to admire his guts. It's amazing how we take things for granted—like being able to walk, or to eat, or to speak—even to go to the bathroom by ourselves. This man was a college student. He could not walk. He could not feed himself. He could barely speak. His wheelchair couldn't fit through the bathroom door, so two of us had to hold him up while he relieved himself. But I never heard him complain, and when the band was playing, you should have seen him move that chair. He never missed a beat."

"After the party," Jonas went on, "we carried each of those chairs back down those stairs and loaded them onto the elevator on the side of the white V.A. bus. I remember the alley was dark. It was a bitter cold night and snow was still falling. As I came down to see them off, the bus driver was busy securing each chair so they wouldn't roll. 'Take good care of these guys,' I told him. 'They gave everything they had.'

"'Yeah,' he said, bitterly, 'defending some damn nameless hill in a country they didn't know, and a stupid war nobody wanted. What more can we ask of them?'"

"The black paraplegic who I had helped at the game was being helped aboard. He was falling asleep, and no doubt drunk. I turned to his wife," Jonas said softly, "and I said, 'I hope you had a great time tonight.' She looked at me, with a tear in her eye, and she said, 'Do you really?'"

"As the bus pulled out of that alley, honey," Jonas said, "I stood there in the dark, and the snow, and the cold—crying like a baby."

"I know, honey," Patty said as she leaned over her husband and planted a kiss on his forehead, "but you did a good thing. You did a lot more than many other people would have done, and it made you feel good, didn't it?"

"I suppose so," Jonas said, "only I wish I could have done more. I wanted so much to do something—to take those beautiful brains out of those broken bodies, and give them new lives."

"Well, honey, who knows?" Patty said. "Someday you just might be able to do that. But, for now, I'd like to see if we can make that dining room light shake again."

"What!" Jonas said, as he looked over at his wife.

"Well," Patty said, "We've only got a week. You can sleep when you get to Peru." She said as she climbed on top of her husband.

CHAPTER V

JONAS

July 29, 2019 dawned like any other day. The sun rose in the east, and would set in the west. It was early winter in the Southern Hemisphere, but in the rainforests of the western Amazon the winter brought only the promise of more rainfall—the afternoon thundershowers to break the heat of the day. However, higher in the Andes the promise of winter was more real, and Hector was anxious to be there. After years of waiting—years of wondering whether or not his theory was correct or just another pipe dream—the answer was coming very soon.

Over seventeen years ago, June 19 and 20, 2002, to be exact, a message had been sent out into space. A mathematical message, consisting of a laser beam and radio transmission, had been aimed at a nearby star—Sirius. At the time, Hector considered it a "distress signal." Ever since then, at the observatory at Huancayo, a lonely, perhaps futile, vigil had been maintained with a skeleton crew. Receivers set at 1420 megahertz; laser receptors ready to record any transmissions from the seemingly endless universe. And so far, as had been expected, there'd been no answer, no transmissions of any kind. 8.56 light years to Sirius and 8.56 light years back. 17.12 light years to send and receive. But now, the time was approaching. Anytime after 7:55 p.m. this evening a message could come, and if it did....

It was too bad, Hector thought, that Jonas couldn't be here, either to gape in amazement, or to scoff, "I told you so," for wasting so much time and money. Poor Jonas, he had dedicated his life to computer science, only to have it turn on him, literally.

An industrial accident they said.

* * *

After his one-year sabbatical to Peru, Jonas had returned home to his wife, his family and his job at Telecom. But he was not the same Jonas. The year in Peru had changed him. He had developed a profound respect for life, and for history, which he had never displayed before. He would write, call, and e-mail messages to Hector, detailing the work he was engaged in, and how it could alter the entire course of human history. Jonas had become obsessed with a newer field of computer science—artificial intelligence. He had even brought his family into it. His daughter, Holly, had become his assistant upon graduating from Columbia.

Jonas believed that if Mankind were ever to break the bonds of planet Earth and reach out into the heavens, he couldn't do so in his flimsy, human body. If, somehow, his intelligence could be transferred temporarily into a more durable container, he could journey to the far corners of the universe without having to worry about time constraints.

Jonas wanted to develop a whole new generation of computers, computers that not only would think like humans, but computers that would actually *be* human. He tried to explain it to Hector one night, during one of their endless telephone conversations.

"Suppose that I, Jonas Larkin, wanted to travel to Sirius," Larkin said to Hector. "I couldn't do it. Do you know why?"

"Do you want me to count the reasons?" Hector laughed.

"I couldn't go because I'm not an astronaut, I'm not in shape, I'm too old—and probably a hundred more reasons I couldn't think of."

"OK, you can't go to Sirius," Hector agreed.

"But," Jonas said, in a quieter, slower delivery, "what if my mind *could* go—without my body?"

"What are you talking about?" Hector said, "You're crazy. This sounds like Frankenstein."

"Sort of," said Jonas, "but hear me out. Suppose we could design a computer that would allow an individual to transfer, for a fixed period of time, his entire human brain function into its memory. Think of it. I'd still be Jonas inside my body, but I'd also be Jonas inside the computer. For all intents and purposes, there would be two of me."

"Right now, Jonas, I think one of you is one too many. You'd better stop smoking those funny cigarettes."

"Hector, listen to me! If this could be done, we could take the computerized 'me' and put it in a spaceship. We could send the spaceship to Sirius, or any place else, for that matter. 'I' would experience all the wonders of space flight, see all the wonders of the universe, visit all the planets 'I' want to, and not have to worry about food, or health, or even time itself. How does that sound?"

"It sounds fantastic, impossible, ridiculous—and—"

"Go on, Hector."

"Frightening, my friend, frightening as hell."

"As frightening, Hector, as sending a signal into space when you don't know what the answer will be?"

"Yes," Hector paused, "I guess you're right. How close are you to doing this?"

"I've got a prototype on the drawing boards now. Holly's helping me, Hec. She's fantastic, a real chip off the old block."

"The question is," Hector shot back, "a block of what? Look, Jonas, you know I wish you well in whatever you decide to do, but this sounds dangerous to me. It's like 'cloning' yourself."

"I suppose you could think that," said Jonas, "but what's the alternative? Suspended animation? Warp drive? If we do find a way to suspend human life, or to travel faster than the speed of light, that will be fine, but I'm not convinced that either is possible. And, if we could use suspended animation, we still have human frailties to deal with once we come out of suspension. As for hyper-light speed, that *is* science fiction. No, Hector, I still think my approach has the best chance of success."

"All right, Jonas," Hector said, "assuming you're correct, what happens when the spaceship comes back to earth and 'you' meet 'you' again?"

"There's the rub, my friend," Jonas replied. "Do we download the computer 'me' back into 'me'? More importantly perhaps, *can* we download the computer 'me' into 'me'? Don't forget I've been living two entirely different lives since separation, and those experiences will overlap each other. My theory is that the brain will treat the new information just like it does any other, which comes in through its senses. It will process it, store it, and recall it. I will remember both sets of memories equally well."

"That's your theory," said Hector, "I hope you can prove it."

"We'll soon know, old friend. I'm also thinking of the medical implications this could have. We may be able to help people with brain and spinal injuries. If we could free them from their wheelchairs, even if only for a short time, wouldn't it be worth it? I know some veterans who sure would think so. What about people with learning disabilities, or multiple personality disorders? Hell, we might be able to "erase" the personalities we didn't want! The possibilities are mind-boggling. You should see what the executives upstairs think of all this. They're ecstatic. They can hardly wait to go public."

"Tell me, Jonas," Hector asked, "what happens if the 'real' you has a terminal illness, or dies before the 'computer' you gets put back in?"

"The same thing that would happen to any computer program no longer needed," Jason replied, "it could be deleted."

"I don't know, Jonas, it sounds to me like the lawyers are going to end up with some very interesting cases before this all settles out."

"They're already on it."

"Well, keep me posted."

"Don't worry, you'll be one of the first to hear. Take care now."

Those were the last words Hector heard from Jonas, "Take care now."

As Hector understood it, things were progressing smoothly as the year 2005 drew to a close. Jonas had been engaged in a major modification of the Telecom 770 to accommodate this new technology. So precisely had he designed this upgrade that eventually it was capable of absorbing all the information stored in a living human brain. The DNA and RNA codes in each brain cell could be scanned and then duplicated in the electrochemical cells of the computer. This was accomplished by using a newly developed super sensitive MRI, magnetic resonance imaging technique which could actually differentiate body cells. In short, the brain of any living person could be duplicated completely, right down to childhood memories, individual experiences, and habits. The computer literally became the person scanned into it. And, since memory was stored in the brain by coding, or imprinting, molecules in brain cells, it might be possible to reverse the process. By connecting a computer to the brain, it might be possible to alter behavior, or to implant knowledge. Research in these areas was already in the planning stages.

Jonas was now confronted with an ethical dilemma. In order to prove his theory, it would be necessary to use a human brain. Connecting a laboratory rat, a guinea pig, or even a chimpanzee to the device would not work because there would be no way to know if the computer actually thought like the rat, the guinea pig, or the chimpanzee.

Although the risks appeared minimal, Jonas couldn't ask someone else to do it. Holly later told Hector that Jonas discussed this problem with Patty and his children, and they all agreed that he had to try. On Tuesday, following the Thanksgiving weekend, Jonas was attached to the scanning MRI device, which would feed the codes to the computer.

As Patty, Holly and Matthew looked on, the procedure appeared to be going as planned. Nearing the end of the scan, there was a momentary power outage, shorter than the blink of an eye.

The monitor screen went blank, and Jonas went into cardiac arrest.

The medical staff on stand-by was able to resuscitate him, but the electroencephalogram showed a flat line. All of Jonas' brain functions were gone. It was as if his entire brain function had vanished into cyberspace.

Hector flew to New York for the funeral, and gave a short eulogy at the service. It was an elaborate affair. Jonas was known and respected throughout the world for his contributions to the computer and telecommunications industries. Hundreds of friends and colleagues attended the ceremony, which was conducted at Immaculate Conception Church in Spring Valley. Hector quoted his friend, when he said, "'A scientist always pursues things to their logical conclusion, and if this is the conclusion you've drawn, you must pursue it.' Jonas pursued his conclusion, and we have learned much because of it. Jonas left this world a better place than he found it, and that's the best that can be said for any man."

Undoubtedly, the most moving part of the ceremony came when Matthew Larkin stepped up to the podium. Matthew, whom the doctors didn't want Patty to have, was a tall handsome young man, with broad shoulders, an athletic build, reddish brown hair and blue eyes. Taking some papers from inside his jacket Matthew began to read. His voice was full, and one could sense the pride and love he held for his father:

"The seasons pass. Winter follows fall, as time inexorably marches on, and Christmas arrives with ruffles and flourishes to proclaim a renewal of faith. Mankind once again pulls down the old, tattered box from the attic, and hangs up his dreams with the ornaments. But the cold winds of January will bring home the realities of life.

"Until the age of eleven my father lived under a misconception. He was white. President Eisenhower was white. The people on TV were white. Dick and Jane were white. When thanksgiving came, and Jonas' class had to draw pictures, all the pilgrims were white. Even the Indians looked white. During the Christmas season, when the local Woolworth's® had its toy sale, all the kids in the neighborhood would tell a white Santa Claus what they wanted.

"However, the teachers who taught my father about the world—they were mostly black. So were his classmates, his neighbors, and his friends. Color didn't seem to matter much to him then. He was only a child. How could he have known that race could become so important as he reached adulthood, that magical age when all would be revealed.

"The Glenville neighborhood of Cleveland was dynamic in the 1950's. Many of the Jews who formerly lived along East 105th Street had moved to Cleveland Heights, or, if they had money, to Beachwood or to Shaker Heights. African-Americans were moving in to replace them, although they weren't called that then. Many of the remaining white residents were transplanted West Virginians who left the coal mines for better-paying jobs in the auto plants, like my grandfather. And, of course, there were native Clevelanders, like my grandmother, who had lived there all their lives.

"Glenville was alive in 1958, and to a young boy of eleven, it was exciting. "In addition to beingexciting, Glenville was also crowded. So much so, in fact, that Jonas' elementary school, Oliver Wendell Holmes, which stood on East 105th Street, was forced to conduct half-day sessions. One winter, my father had to walk several blocks to old Glenville High School to attend fifth-grade class in the basement. He and his classmates looked like midgets compared to the 'grownups' upstairs.

"Looking back on those times, Dad said there were three close friends who were to influence him for the rest of his life.

"Aaron was a short, pudgy, black-haired, brown-eyed Jewish boy who lived in an apartment over on the next block. He attended Hebrew school, so they were not classmates. They played after school and on weekends. Aaron was a good person, a true 'froind', as his mother would say. Her parents were always gentle and kind to Dad. They introduced him to corned beef, a craving for which I can honestly say he was never able to satisfy. They spoke with a funny accent, and Aaron explained that his family had come here from Germany.

"Kenny was Dad's second friend. He was Chinese, with dark hair, a ready smile, and that rare ability to show comradeship, which was truly genuine. Kenny had no father and no siblings. He lived with his mother in two rooms in the old Clair-Doan Hotel building, near the corner of St. Clair Avenue and East 105th Street. His mother worked in a small hand laundry. She spoke no English, and whenever Dad visited Kenny, he would translate everything that was said so that she could understand. From these 'conversations', Dad learned that Kenny's mother had left China just before Kenny was born, in 1949. This made Kenny two years younger than Dad, so although they attended the same school, they were not in the same class.

"Damon, Dad's third friend, was black. They were the same age, eleven, and they were in the same class at school. Damon sat next to Jonas in the third row. They studied together, played together during recess, and it was not merely coincidence that their grades on papers would sometimes be identical. Unlike Aaron or Kenny, Damon lived several blocks away, near East 110th Street, so they could not be together after school. During Summer, however, they would get together to play, or for things like bottle collecting, or selling Kool-Aid® with Dad's sister, Ruthie.

"While playing, the kids would often talk about themselves, or the people around them, and the one thing they all agreed on was that adults were strange people. Take Aaron's folks for example. Although Aaron's father was a kind man, there was an air about him, an uneasiness, which Dad never overcame. He was not very talkative, and he walked with a bad limp. One day, while eating lunch at Aaron's Dad asked Aaron why his father walked 'funny.' Aaron looked at his mother, but did not answer.

"'In the war,' was her short, terse reply. Aaron's mother, a slight woman with dark hair, brown eyes, and usually wearing a smile, was not smiling now. She presented an appearance, which Dad had never seen before. She was deep in thought and her eyes seemed to be staring through the kitchen wall. It frightened him a little. Dad decided never to ask any more questions about 'the war' in Aaron's house again.

"And then there was Kenny. One day, while playing in his apartment, Dad happened to ask him about his father. Kenny answered, 'He got killed in a war, back home in China.' Kenny gave his mother an immediate translation. She then told Kenny something in a quiet but firm voice. 'We have to go out now; Mom's got things to do,' he said, starting for the door.

"As he and Dad were leaving, Dad couldn't help noticing the expression on her face. Her eyes were penetrating, and her smile had faded into despair. 'You know, Kenny,' he said, as they galloped down the stairs, 'sometimes your Mom looks like Aaron's.'

"One Saturday, after a profitable bottle hunt, Damon and my Dad decided to go to the movies together. Saturday matinee—double feature—'Godzilla' and 'Rodan.' Unfortunately, there was one problem Damon and Jonas didn't think of. Dad lived on East 102nd Street, and Damon lived near East 110th. However, the theatre was on Hayden Avenue in East Cleveland. Jonas thought it would be nothing for his Dad to take them both there in his car, just as he often did with Jonas and his sister, Ruthie. This time his Dad said no. Damon's parents refused him also. When Jonas asked his Dad why, he said, 'It's the wrong neighborhood.'

"'Then how come you take Ruthie and me there?' Jonas asked. It was then that Dad explained. 'Wrong' really meant 'white.' Damon might not be welcome.

"Damon and Jonas couldn't understand this at all. They were friends. They were classmates. No two people look exactly alike, so why did their parents place so much emphasis on the fact that *they* were different.

"Damon and Dad never got to see 'Godzilla' together.

"Shortly thereafter, Dad's family moved to the Collinwood neighborhood. Aaron, Kenny and Damon gave way to new friends and new relationships. Dad never heard from Aaron and Kenny again. But, he did hear something about Damon.

"Twelve years later, in 1970, Dad was home on military leave for the Christmas season. He was grown up now, and it was his turn to learn about war. One evening, while awaiting his flight overseas, there was a late-night news broadcast on television. The weekly Vietnam casualty report was airing. Local boy killed. PFC, Army—his picture—his family—probably taken on some happy occasion—high school graduation, perhaps. And, inevitably, his mother, with her ready smile, and that sense of pride that all mothers show when their children are fully-grown.

"But, as in countless generations before, Aaron's mother, Kenny's mother, and now Damon's mother, could only stare in bewilderment, could only cry softly, and ask humbly, 'Why?'

"In 1988, a veteran walked up to the Vietnam Veterans Memorial. He found Damon's name. He scribbled a little note, and placed it on the ground in front. The note read, 'Sorry we couldn't go to the movies together, Damon.' He signed it 'Jonas'. He then tearfully saluted, and walked away.

"And the seasons pass. Winter follows fall, as time inexorably marches on, and Christmas arrives with ruffles and flourishes to proclaim a renewal of faith. But the cold winds of January bring home the realities of life. Mankind once again packs away his dreams of brotherhood, peace and love together with all the Christmas decorations. As he places the tattered old box back in the attic for another year—somewhere, lies a snow-covered field. The rows of white crosses stand tall in the shadow of a setting sun. The bitter cold wind tears at a woman's sorrowed face. The silence is broken by a distant bugle sounding 'Taps,' and a tear trickles down her cheek.

There was brief pause. Except for some barely audible crying, there was complete silence. Matthew then resumed:

"My father lived for the day when all men would be equal. He lived for a time when the world would be at peace. He dedicated his life to improving all our lives. That is the *true* measure of greatness. Dad was a great man. I'm going to miss you, Dad.

Matthew hugged his mother and sister. There wasn't a dry eye in the house.

The following year, in 2006, Jonas was awarded a Nobel Prize, posthumously, for his revolutionary work in telecommunications. The first working model of his 770 computer was donated to the Smithsonian. Holly continued to work for Telecom.

Matthew published several articles about his father's life, with Hector collaborating on their work together in Peru. Patty kept their house in Spring Valley. She opened a small antique shop, featuring Victorian-style interior decorating. Patty also continued to teach part-time. It helped, to keep herself busy, she said.

CHAPTER VI

PUCALLPA

Now, nine years later, Hector could look back on the work he and Jonas had done together. "The year from Hell," Jonas would often refer to it, half jokingly.

To begin with there was the location. Huancayo lies about six hours east of Lima along the Central Highway, or "Trail" as Jonas called it. To get there one must cross over the Ticlio Pass at an altitude of 15,500 feet. With a population of about one hundred thousand, Huancayo itself lies at an altitude of 10,500 feet. It took several days just to get used to the thin air. Huancayo was a major mining and trade center. The Mantaro Valley produced wheat, corn, potatoes and barley. Silver and copper were mined nearby and there wasa large smelter located at La Oroya. The *Observatorio Geomagnetico de Huancayo* was a major facility for studying geology in the Andes.

Hector also liked to remind Jonas that Huancayo had the distinction of having the most UFO sightings in the Western Hemisphere.

The thing Hector remembered most was, that although Jonas always held a certain degree of skepticism about Hector's theory, Jonas never let it interfere with his work. From the moment Jonas first landed in Lima and all during the torturous move to Huancayo, he never complained. If equipment arrived damaged he didn't explode. It was almost as if he expected it to, so he'd shrug it off. If a computer program didn't run as it was supposed to, Jonas would work on it until it did. Hector remembered that Jonas once quipped, "If we could only get computers to do what we want them to do, instead of what we program them to do, things surely would run a lot smoother around here."

From Huancayo, the equipment had to be transported another two hundred miles to Pucallpa. This was accomplished by using small transport planes and trucks. Some equipment was hauled in by using 3,000-ton vessels from Iquitos, downstream on the Amazon River. Again, Jonas worked with machine-like precision. Hector had to admire him.

Unlike Huancayo, high in the Andes, where, in July, winter in the Southern Hemisphere, temperatures can drop to minus ten degrees Fahrenheit, Pucallpa steamed on the Ucayali River in the hot, humidAmazonian rain forest of eastern Peru. Founded in 1534, Pucallpa remained isolated until 1945, when the 526-mile Lima-Pucallpa highway was completed. A frontier community, equipped with electricity, Pucallpa lacked paved streets and sewers in many areas. In addition to being a market for local agricultural produce, Pucallpa was an industrial center, with sawmills and plants for extracting rosewood oil—tragically a major center for deforestation of the Amazon basin. A petroleum refinery was at the terminus of a 47-mile long pipeline from the Ganzo Azul oil fields in Huanuco. Numerous missionary groups had headquarters in and around Pucallpa, and the area had undergone rapid colonization. The population in 1990 was estimated to be 153,000, but had undoubtedly increased since. One couldn't possibly get farther from the gleaming towers of Manhattan than Pucallpa, Peru.

Heat and humidity are a computer's worst nightmare. Those and power outages. Maintaining the computer room at a constant temperature of 70 degrees Fahrenheit and fifty-percent humidity, without having the power shut off, proved to be the biggest challenge Jonas had to face. It was a never-ending battle. "Murphy's Law," Jonas would say, "became Murphy's Constant." In order to keep ahead of these problems, Jonas installed back-up systems everywhere he could think of. Back-up generators were installed on the back-up generators if the power failed, with circuit protectors on the circuit protectors. He installed air conditioning units to back-up the air conditioning units, with dehumidifiers just in case. Everything was done in duplicate. Every computer program installed in the hard drives had back-up programs on disk. Nothing, Jonas thought, would be left to chance.

Still, there were those moments, those almost infinitely short, but agonizingly long, moments, when one system failed, and the back-up kicked in, or didn't, which "tried men's souls."

Glitches they were called, and glitches they were. They couldn't be eliminate. "All you can do is build enough back-up to minimize the damage—hopefully." That was "Jonas' Law".

"How ironic," thought Hector, "it was just such a glitch that probably killed Jonas. What good was all that back-up then?" Jonas knew the risks. Perhaps that's why he couldn't ask anyone else to do what he wouldn't do himself. That was Jonas' Law, too.

Hector remembered that he had once asked Jonas why, if he wasn't absolutely convinced of Hector's theory, he'd agreed to come to Peru anyway? He never forgot Jonas' answer. "Think of Pasteur," Jonas said. "Everyone thought he was crazy when he talked about diseases being caused by micro-organisms, and the need for sterile technique in surgical procedures. How could tiny little creatures, barely visible to the eye, possibly kill a human being. In many ways, Pasteur was like a space explorer, only his universe was micro-space, the inner world. Pasteur believed that there were countless forms of organisms living in the micro-world, which couldn't be seen, or even detected, by contemporary means; but that didn't stop him from searching. The later discovery of viruses confirmed his theory. So, Hector, what's so crazy about looking out to macro-space, and looking for life on other worlds in the universe? It's logical. It makes sense, but...."

"But what?"

"Pasteur discovered that there were two kinds of micro-organisms, Hec. Those that produced disease, and others that didn't. Some even proved helpful. I just hope that if we do find someone out there, we discover the latter, and not the former."

During the years of waiting for the return signal, Hector had plenty of time to think about the signal he and Jonas had sent, and what the response might be. Jonas was never completely convinced that there would be a return signal, but Hector was always confident. As the intervening years went by, Hector had ample opportunity to study still more of the ancient artifacts and inscriptions. The more he studied the more he became convinced that the source of the ancient deities lay somewhere beyond Earth. While it was possible that the similarities between the cultures of America and those of the Near East could be attributed to Egyptians carrying their knowledge to the New World by boat, as Heyerdahl speculated, and as Hector himself had demonstrated by finding the Egyptian scroll, there were still too many puzzling questions.

There was still no satisfactory explanation for the 900 giant stone monoliths (100 still standing) on Easter Island, each staring toward the heavens. Scientists were still trying to explain it away by saying that the native population had de-forested the island making various tools and moving devices needed to haul the giant carvings, each weighing twenty tons or more, from the inland quarries to their locations near the shore. In the process they had destroyed their food supply and either died off, or were forced to abandon the island. In an endeavor to prove their theory, an "exact" duplicate statue was made in the 1990's. All attempts to move it by known means, using materials that might have been available back then, ended in failure, because moving the statue scarred its surface. There were no scars on the ancient statues. Furthermore, there was the problem of cutting the stone. The statues were made of volcanic rock, extremely hard and nearly impossible to cut. How could the natives so skillfully cut the statues with only the primitive tools found on the island.

There was also the mystery of cotton. Scientists had proven years ago that American cotton was a hybrid between a wild, native, American plant and one, which grew along the Nile in ancient Egypt. Their conclusion raised a new question. How did the Nile cotton get to America? Salt water kills it, so the seeds couldn't be carried over by currents. Wind couldn't do it, either, for several reasons. First, the seeds would have to be separated from the cotton balls, which any cotton picker would testify, is not easy. Second, cottonseeds are round; they are not aerodynamic, and cannot be spread by wind. Third, and most important, the prevailing winds would not carry them into the Southern Hemisphere anyway. Birds couldn't bring the seeds, either, because no known species would touch the cotton ball, which contains the seeds. One could rule out the Vikings or King Dan I of Denmark as well. Cold weather also kills cotton. This would seem to leave the Egyptians themselves as the only candidates, but there was another question. If the Egyptians brought the cotton, and taught the natives to grow it, why didn't they teach them how to use it? Not one loom had ever been found. Why, then, did the Incas grow cotton? Who and what was it for?

The Egyptians must have brought bananas along as well. Bananas were not native to the Western Hemisphere, and they did not propagate by seeds. Rather, they reproduced by sending out runners, or underground stems, which grew into new trees. Even the heartiest banana tree couldn't send a runner across the Atlantic Ocean.

The theory that the Egyptians were responsible still troubled Hector. The fact that a few boatloads of Egyptians sailing across the Atlantic Ocean could have forged a culture as advanced as the Incas in so short a time, having only illiterate savages to begin with, seemed incredible to him. Furthermore, if western cultures owed their existence to those in the east, then where did the eastern cultures come from?

Of all the evidence Hector had studied during the past twenty-five years, the one piece which offered the greatest support for his theory had to be the Piri Reis maps.

Piri Reis (1468-1554) was a Turkish admiral. In the early eighteenth century two of his atlases had been discovered in the Topkapi Palace at Istanbul. These atlases, dating to 1513 contained maps showing the East Coast of South America, the West Coast of Africa, as well as the coast of Antarctica. Piri Reis could not have acquired his information on Antarctica from contemporary sources because Antarctica remained undiscovered until 1818, more than three hundred years after he drew the map!

By comparing the angles and distortions factors, Hector confirmed that the Piri Reis maps had to be Copies of aerial photographs taken from an altitude of at least 5,000 miles! The coastal markings of Antarctica, which hadn't been discovered yet, were remarkably accurate. They even showed rock formations buried under ice for centuries, which could only be detected by echo-sounding equipment! Interior features of the continent were accurately drawn, although it was impossible for men to have set foot in many of these places. There was more. The ice-free coast of Queen Maud Land was also shown on the map. This coast had not been ice-free since about 4,000 BC. Although it would be impossible to determine exactly the earliest date that such a feat could have been accomplished, it would seem that the Queen Maud Land littoral must have remained in a stable, unglaciated state for at least 9,000 years before the ice-cap spread over it. There was no known civilization that had the ability or need to survey this coastline in that time period,13,000 BC to 4,000 BC. This time frame fit Hector's theory perfectly, that the ancient gods were in fact alien astronauts.

The sudden appearance of highly advanced cultures in diverse areas of the world now could be explained. There had to be an initial starting point—a "laboratory" where the aliens could experiment and condition the primitives into becoming the future rulers of the Earth. From this initial training camp the aliens would then transport groups of "guinea pigs", each similarly equipped, to different locations on Earth. The most convenient way to accomplish this was by air transport, which would explain the belief held by ancient civilizations that they were descended from flying gods in the heavens.

This would also explain the need for aerial maps. The aliens would need to have detailed studies of climate and terrain in order to locate ideal environments for their experimental colonies. Some sites they selected included the Tigris and Euphrates river basin of modern day Iraq, the Indus Valley of modern India, the Yellow River basin of China, Central America and northern South America, and, of course, the Nile Valley in Egypt. By placing groups of individuals into these differing, but habitable, environments, so remote from each other that early contact between them would be impossible, the aliens could observe how these creatures would adapt to their environments and develop their own, unique cultures, given the same initial training.

It reminded Hector of his work in a microbiology laboratory, when he worked as a laboratory assistant in graduate school. He would take several samples of the same bacterial culture and place each sample on a petri dish containing a different culture medium.

He would then observed the dishes to see which ones stimulated growth of the bacteria, or which ones slowed or even inhibited growth.

Hector also believed that once the aliens were reasonably certain that the cultures would survive, the aliens departed in order to allow the cultures to progress on their own. The aliens may have hinted of returning at some future time, but actually had no intention of doing so. What the aliens hoped for was that as the cultures developed, they would eventually come in contact with each other. They would compete with each other for the limited resources on Earth, with one dominant culture finally winning out. Perhaps one day in the far distant future, that culture would reach out to the stars just as these aliens had done. This was the plan the aliens had envisioned, as Hector perceived it.

But, where was this "initial starting point", this so-called "laboratory" where the aliens performed their wondrous miracles? Was it just a figment of Hector's imagination, or did it exist? And, if it existed, where would the aliens have built it? Would there be any traces left behind to show its existence, or would the aliens deliberately destroy the site, in order to cover the fact that they'd been here?

Hector and Jonas had pondered these questions during their months in Peru, and the conclusion they had reached was as astounding as anything either man could have imagined when they met that first time back in New York.

Hector's theory hinged on one all-important aspect—the existence, or former existence of an alien settlement which they used as a base of operations for their experiments. Contemporary scientists argued that the ancient civilizations had developed in Asia and Africa, spreading later to Central and South America. The evidence seemed to point that way. Heyerdahl's work, the King Dan legend, cultural and architectural similarities, even cotton and bananas supported it. However, Hector postulated, if flight was used by the aliens to establish their colonies, then their base of operations could have been anywhere on Earth.

About six months after Jonas had arrived in Peru, while working together in the computer room one day, Hector said, "Jonas, may I ask a hypothetical question?"

"Shoot," Larkin replied as he checked some printouts.

"If you were the alien, and you came to Earth for the first time with the intention of establishing a base that might be needed for several thousand years, where would you build it?"

Larkin had replied, "If I were the alien I think that initially I'd want to be as inconspicuous as possible. I'd want to keep the Earth as pristine as I could. I'd pick a spot that was remote, but with a moderate climate, with no extremes of hot or cold."

"OK," Hector said, "you've just ruled out all the populated areas as well as the Polar regions. What's left?"

"Well," Larkin responded, "If it were me, I'd pick an island someplace—an uninhabited island far removed from the mainland, and far removed from other islands. The island would have to be geologically stable, free of earthquakes and volcanoes. I'd also assume that the aliens are biologically similar to us, so they'd need water and food. The island would have to be large enough to support the base, and also big enough for spaceships to land on. Obviously the aliens would be rotating crews, and re-supplying the base. Spaceships would land and take off at regular intervals. They wouldn't want the earthly natives to see this activity, so I would imagine the island would be very isolated."

"My thoughts exactly," Hector said. "What if I could show you such a place? It's about 2300 miles from the nearest continent, and nearly that far from the nearest island. It's about 117 square miles in size, and it's warm throughout the year. The island was created by volcanic activity, but the volcanoes are extinct, and in fact, serve as excellent reservoirs for rainwater. The soil is fertile, so crops could be grown if needed. What do you think?"

"I'd say we ought to check it out."

"Pack your bags. We leave tomorrow."

CHAPTER VII

RAPA NUI

Rapa Nui (Spanish Isla de Pascua) is a triangular shaped island belonging to Chile, about 2,300 miles west of the Chilean coast. The island was formed by three extinct volcanoes. Strong trade winds keep the island warm throughout the year. The indigenous vegetation includes grasses, but sugarcane, sweet potatoes, taro roots and tropical fruits have been introduced. Fresh water collects in the three crater lakes. Although Polynesians probably settled the island around 400 AD, it was not discovered by Europeans until a Dutch explorer landed in 1722. Chile annexed the island in 1888. The western end of the island is reserved for the indigenous population of about 2,100. The eastern part of the island is used for grazing by sheep and cattle, which were introduced by European settlers and the Chileans.

A s Hector and Jonas flew over the island on a sunny January day, 2002, they could observe the general topography. Although hilly, the island was not overly mountainous, and generally devoid of trees. "According to legend," Hector explained to Jonas as their plane circled the island, "about 1,500 years ago a Polynesian chief named Hotu Matu'a ("The Great Parent") sailed here in a double canoe from another Polynesian island with his family. The Polynesians were great navigators and sailed to many islands throughout the Pacific. Hotu Matu'a landed over here on Anakena Beach. He called the island 'Te-Pito-te-Henua', which means 'end of the land', or 'land's end'."

Of course, Larkin thought as they continued circling. This island has yet another, much more famous name. The Dutch explorer, Captain Jacob Roggeveen coined it when he landed in 1722, because he landed on Easter Day. So, Jonas, this is Easter Island, home of the giant stone megaliths called *Moai*. This is Hector's alien base!

Jonas and Hector spent several days on Easter Island, exploring it from one end to the other. Hector had visited the island previously as part of his research, and had spent many weeks studying the megaliths, the topography of the island, and taking photographs of the wooden tablets, which appeared to have writings carved into them. This was very important, because it was the only known source of evidence of a form of writing in all Polynesia! While hiking over the island Hector lectured incessantly about what he knew of the island, and of its earlier inhabitants.

"Ever since Europeans learned of the island's existence, there has been debate about the origin of the isolated native population found here. There were several thousand on the island when the Dutch captain landed, but that number dwindled to about two hundred by the late 1800's. This was followed by an influx of Chileans, and some intermarriage took place. The question is, did the native population sail originally from the east, from South America, or from Polynesia to the north and west? In either case, the voyage would have been daunting. To reach Easter Island by sailboat would require a minimum of two weeks, covering over two thousand miles of seemingly endless ocean. The original inhabitants would have to be of a sea-faring culture, capable of building long-voyaging craft.

"When they landed on Easter Island is also in debate. Linguists have them arriving from East Polynesia about 400 AD. Archaeological findings suggested 700 to 800 AD, but it was also known that people in Melanesia were voyaging in boats and trading with natives on other islands as early as 5,500 BC! The linguists pointed out the similarities in culture and language seen on various islands throughout Polynesia, extending over thousands of square miles, as evidence of a common origin. They also had genetic evidence. In 1994, DNA from a dozen Easter Island skeletons was tested and found to be of Polynesian origin.

"One thing was certain, wherever they came from, when they landed on Rapa Nui these early settlers brought plants with them to cultivate in their new home. Evidence suggests that those plants included banana trees, taro root and sweet potatoes. Therein was still another mystery, namely, the sweet potato. Botanists had proven that the sweet potato originated in South America. If so, how could Polynesians, journeying from west to east, have brought it with them?

"Thor Heyerdahl was convinced that people from pre-Inca Peru voyaged east to west, driven by the westerly trade winds and currents directly to Rapa Nui. He proved it in 1947 with his historic journey on the Kon Tiki, drifting 4,300 miles across the Pacific, east to west for three months, before running aground on the Polynesian island of Puka Puka. Heyerdahl further supported his theory by pointing out similarities in the construction of stone walls on Rapa Nui and those of the Incas."

Hector pointed out these walls to Jonas on their tour of the island. Hector quoted Captain Cook "'The workmanship is not inferior to the best plain piece of masonry we have in England. They use no sort of cement; yet the joints are exceedingly close, and the stones morticed and tenanted one into another in a very artful manner.'"

"Sounds like Incas to me," Jonas replied.

"It is," Hector asserted. "I think the Polynesians actually reached South America, and made contact with the Peruvians. Then, sometime later, the Polynesians headed west, carrying the sweet potato with them, and landed on Rapa Nui. Either they learned the stone-cutting techniques from the Peruvians, or the Peruvians visited them still later, or both. This explains the Polynesian origin, the sweet potato and the stone-cutting all at once."

"I'm sold," said Jonas. "You've covered the 'where'. The 'when' is a bit shaky; but, the 'why' is still a complete mystery."

"Let me continue," Hector lectured on.

"With the introduction of the sweet potato, the population on Rapa Nui expanded greatly. Sweet potatoes are a low maintenance high-energy food source. Between 1,000 and 1,600 AD the population on Rapa Nui might have reached as high as 10,000. This coincides with the time during which the moai were being carved and hauled to their final resting places on top of the 'ahu.' 'Ahu' has two meanings to the Easter Island culture. An ahu is the flat pedestal, about four feet high, upon which the moai stand, usually six or seven moai per ahu. 'Ahu' can also refer to the entire sacred ceremonial site itself. For example, 'Ahu Akivi' would be an ahu site with seven moai standing.

"After 1,600 AD, the entire culture of Rapa Nui collapsed. Although once covered with forest, the island became totally barren of trees. The soil was depleted from over-cultivation and erosion. Ecological suicide was the result. Overpopulation, food shortages, death, perhaps even cannibalism, resulted. All work on the Moai stopped, and by the time the Dutch arrived in 1722, only 122 years later, they found a barren landscape, a few thousand Polynesians still living, and hundreds of stone giants staring into the heavens.

"All right," Jonas said. "We now have the 'when'. That leaves 'why' and I presume you have an answer for that, as well?" Jonas asked, somewhat sarcastically, knowing that Hector was about to launch into another lecture.

"To understand why, Jonas," Hector explained, "we first have to understand 'what'. Just exactly what were these megaliths? Let's observe one up close."

As they slowly walked up to one of the sleeping stone giants, Jonas was utterly amazed. Its shear size and proportions were astounding, and yet, there was an aura of peaceful serenity about it.

Hector resumed, "Jonas, have you ever heard of Dr. Jo Anne Van Tilberg?"

"No, I don't believe I have," Jonas replied.

"Well, Jonas, she's a famous archaeologist and she devoted fifteen years of painstaking effort to inventory, catalogue and measure each of the moai statues. Her work is a masterpiece, and I had the opportunity to meet her. This is what she found out.

"The 'average' moai stood 13.29 feet tall. Its width at its base was 5.25 feet, and at its head was 4.86 feet. Its depth through its body at midpoint was 3.02 feet and its total volume was 210.48 cubic feet. Its center of gravity was 4.46 feet. However, the most telling feature of all was its weight. The 'average' moai weighed 13.78 tons, or 27,560 pounds! And, as if this weren't impressive enough, there were 887 moai known to exist on Easter Island. Their combined weight would exceed 12,223 tons, or nearly 24,500,000pounds!

"Imagine," Hector said, "taking a World War I battleship, cutting it up by hand into 900 fourteen-ton pieces, and then hauling each piece for miles, perhaps, over dry land, using lumber, rope and human muscle alone. I'd say that's a rough approximation of what these people were trying to accomplish.

"Some of the individual moai were equally, if not more impressive. The smallest standing moai, known as Poike, stood only 3.76 feet high. The larger moai were divided into three categories. The largest moai, which ever stood erect before it toppled over, was "Paro". Paro stood 32.63 feet and weighed 82 tons. The largest moai to have fallen while being erected was unnamed. It measured 33.10 feet and weighed nearly the same. The largest moai ever attempted lies unfinished in Rano Raraku Quarry. Named "El Gigante" its height measures 71.93 feet, and its finished weight would have been approximately 145-165 tons!

"Of the 887 moai known to exist, 288 (32%) were successfully transported to their ahu locations. The Rano Raraku quarry contains 397 (45%) in various stages of completion. The remaining 92 (10%) are lying 'In transit' outside the quarry, and were in the process of being hauled to their ahu locations when they were abandoned.

"That's the 'what', Jonas," Hector said. "*Now* we come to the 'why'.

"I want you to imagine," Hector spoke to Jonas, as they walked beside one of the ahu locations, "you're a Polynesian sailor adrift on the Pacific Ocean at around, say, 950 AD. About two weeks ago you set sail from the Peruvian coast. Some time earlier, you had reached Peru after sailing across the Pacific. Other Polynesians have also reached as far as Hawaii and New Zealand, so this is not surprising. While in Peru, you learned how the Incas cut stone. You have also brought with you some sweet potatoes and some banana trees, which are carefully stored in your canoes. Your intention is to sail west across the Pacific, back to your native islands. Once home, you will share the wonders you have seen with the other people on your island.

Unfortunately, two to three weeks into your voyage, you come upon a strange, unknown island, sitting by itself in the middle of the Pacific. You decide to come ashore, and as you do, what do you see?"

"Enlighten me," Jonas shot back, half amused.

"You see," said Hector, now in a much softer, deliberate tone. "You see the equivalent of Kennedy Space Center!"

"What?" cried Jonas. "Kennedy Space Center on Easter Island! Well, now I *have* heard everything. How far do you plan to go with this story?

"Equivalent, Jason" Hector fired back. "Not Kennedy Space Center itself, but an equivalent base--only much more sophisticated, of course."

"Of course," said Jonas. "Go on."

"This base," Hector continued, "contains all the scientific and technological facilities the aliens need for their studies. There's a research station, communications center, housing for the staff, and, of course, aircraft facilities for helicopters and planes to take off and land. These would be used to ferry workers to different locations on Earth. There would also be a space facility for launching shuttle craft back and forth from the aliens' home planet or some other location in space."

"Naturally," Jonas injected.

"Now," Hector speculated, "put yourself in the place of that primitive Polynesian sailor, watching as helicopters take off or space shuttles lift off into space. Imagine you are watching giant vehicles seemingly move by themselves or listening as these creatures communicate with each other without even seeing each other. Imagine seeing tall buildings reaching up into the sky with giant bowls on top, or metal towers with small flashing stars (lights) on them. What would you think if you were that Polynesian native?"

"Well, Hector," Jonas said, "I guess if I were that primitive man I'd think these creatures were gods."

"Precisely right, Jonas," Hector said, "And what do you think the aliens would do once they discovered the Polynesians?"

"Well, the aliens had to know they were coming long before they reached the island. Surely the aliens had radar... or something."

"Yes, go on."

"There's no way that the humans could warn anyone else about the aliens—being so far away. Besides, who'd believe them, anyway? On the other hand, there would also be no reason for the aliens to harm the humans. They posed no threat. My guess is that the aliens simply let them come."

"And?"

"They let the humans come. When the humans saw the island inhabited by mighty gods, they were afraid to leave for fear that they might anger the gods."

"Either that, or the humans stayed because they were curious. Curiosity can be a very strong force," Hector said.

"Perhaps," Jonas agreed. "In either event, the humans stayed. The aliens observed them but did not interfere with their society. The humans planted bananas and sweet potatoes, built huts, fished—and, probably, began worshiping the aliens as their gods."

"Anything else?"

"The humans began carving stone images of their gods, and placed them upright, facing the heavens, because that's where they came from?"

"That part I'm not so sure of," Hector interrupted. "My theory is that when the aliens packed up and left, the natives began carving the statues as monuments to their gods. I believe that the statues are representations of what the aliens actually looked like. The variance in sizes may reflect the relative importance of each of these gods to the native population. I also believe that these statues were placed at various locations to signify where the alien installations may have been. I think the natives were hoping that the aliens would return one day. In the meantime, these statues would serve as reminders of their visitand welcoming beacons should they ever come back."

"Well", Jason said, "it certainly fits, I suppose, if one believes it. But, tell me, Hector, how come no one has ever found any evidence of alien presence on this island? You know, an alien 'Coke®' bottle, or something else left behind?"

"They were extremely thorough when they packed up. They probably handled it like a surgical procedure. Every 'sponge' was counted. Every nut and bolt accounted for. Remember, Jonas, they didn't want anyone to know they'd ever been here. Which, by the way, leads me to the conclusion that the statues were started *after* they left. Think about it, Jonas. With the exception of those building projects required for defense or protection, nearly all the great works built by man from ancient times through medieval and even up to modern times have been devoted to religion. Whether you talk about the pyramids, the Acropolis, the Aztec temples, Notre Dame, or even the moai on Easter Island, they are all dedicated to worshiping someone out there.

"Well, Hec, I must say that your theory fits into a very nice package. Of course, the critics will argue that because there's no evidence that aliens ever visited the island, there's no way to prove your theory."

"True, but there's no way to disprove it, either. Some things just have to be taken on faith."

"Don't go getting religious on me now, Hec. We're supposed to be men of science."

"Yes, but there's nothing wrong with using science to prove religion, or using religion to prove science, for that matter."

"Yes," Jonas nodded. "But science requires proof. Religion requires faith. This reminds me of the great debate between the creationists and the evolutionists, which occurred all through the 1900's, and still does."

"Yes," Hector said. "I remember the great debates we had when I was in grad school. Personally, I never had a problem reconciling the two."

"Well, we had some dandy discussions," Jonas said. "The problem was that neither side would give in. We were both convinced we were right. I guess that's why our longest and bloodiest wars have been fought over religion. How did you resolve it?

"It's really quite simple once you get past the seven day problem. Obviously, God couldn't create the heavens and Earth in six twenty-four hour days. The Earth didn't even exist yet."

"That's certainly true," said Jonas. "Go on." With each passing day he was becoming more fascinated than ever with the brilliant mind of his colleague.

"Well, Jonas, as God dictated the Bible to his scribes on Earth, he had to keep the story of the Creation short, and he had to keep it simple. Man was still very primitive. Eventually, the time would come whenhe would be ready to learn the details, but this was not the time. The important things to know were these: first, the entire process took place in seven phases; and, second, these phases followed one another in a specific order."

"I'm with you so far."

"God chose to call each phase a *day*, because *day* was easy to understand. He could have used *month* or *year* or any other time period, but he chose *day* probably because there were seven days in a week and seven phases in the process. Keep it simple. He also knew that each *day* would vary in length from other *days*. One might be five billion years long, while another might only be a few thousand. It didn't matter, because man would learn this later, anyway."

"It makes sense." Jonas, gazed at a Moai, that stared toward the heavens.

"As for the order of the seven phases, God dictated that in Genesis. In the beginning there is void, absolute nothingness."

"Phase one," Hector continued, "is the creation of energy—light.

"Phase two is the creation of the basic chemical elements and molecules from energy throughout the universe—the Big Bang, perhaps.

"Phase three is the creation of compounds from the basic chemical elements and molecules throughout the universe, and the formation of galaxies, stars, planets—the Earth among them—and moons.

"Phase four is the development of complex compounds, and the creation of microorganisms capable of reproducing themselves—God uses 'seeds' to keep it simple.

"Phase five is the development of more complex life forms to inhabit all areas of the Earth—evolution if you will, culminating in:

"Phase six, the ascent of man as the highest and most complex life form on Earth.

"Phase seven..."

Jonas interrupted, "And on the seventh day God rested."

"Not quite," Hector continued. "Phase seven, which is on-going, sees the entire process running on its own with God observing what He has done and what mankind is doing—fine tuning when necessary."

"Fine tuning?" asked Jonas.

"That's the term I like to use," said Hector. "The Roman Catholic Church refers to them as *miracles*."

"I see," said Jonas. "And what does the Church say about evolution?"

"As I see it, Jonas, evolution is not contrary to creation. Rather, it is a tool, which God uses to create all the diversity of life on Earth. Science doesn't repudiate Genesis. It confirms it. The more we study the Earth and the universe, the more we see that this is the order in which the process must have occurred. The fact that other ancient writings show creation in this order confirms it," concluded Hector as he and Jonas walked back to their rooms to pack for the return journey to Huancayo.

There would be several other trips during the time when preparations were being made for the transmission. One such trip involved visiting another Peruvian town called Nazca. On that trip, Hector explained his theory about the Nazca glyphs:

"Nazca lies about 300 miles south of Lima on the Pan-American Highway. A town of approximately 30,000 people, Nazca is near the Pacific Coast at an altitude of about 1,000 feet. It is a major tourist center because of the famous "Nazca Lines." They are best seen in an aerial survey of the plains of Nazca, where the Incas created giant glyphs, which can only be seen from high altitudes, and other earthworks, which appear to be airstrips. The reasons for drawing these artifacts have baffled scientists ever since their discovery.

"It's my theory," Hector explained, as they flew above the plain, "that these glyphs are a gigantic drawing, much like the ones early man painted on the walls of his cave. They are drawn on a much larger scale because the story they tell is so immense that it could only be told on a drawing board this big."

"So, if I understand you," Larkin said, gazing down at the plain, "you don't buy the story that this is a landing strip for aliens, as Daniken hypothesized?"

"Certainly not," Hector replied. "I think it's a *picture* of a landing strip"

"A *picture* of a landing strip?" Jonas shot back. "What's the difference?"

"The difference, Jonas, is that the Incas didn't build this because they wanted the aliens to land here. The difference *is* that they wanted to leave behind a record of something they had seen—perhaps far away. I believe the drawing on the plain of Nazca is a crude layout of the alien base on Easter Island!"

"Sometimes, Hec," Jonas fired back, "I wonder why I ever let you drag me into this? I suppose you have a logical explanation for the spider and the bird, drawings, as you call them, which can only be seen from a high altitude."

"Yes, I do," Hector replied. "I believe they are either decals which were painted on the alien aircraft, much as we do to our airplanes today, or..."

"Or what?" Larkin asked, anxious to know the answer.

"The bird is an Incan interpretation of a large airplane. To them, an airplane would look like a giant bird."

"Fine, but what about the spider?"

"Have you ever seen a large military helicopter when it's parked on the ground? Imagine one with eight rotor blades. When parked, the blades don't stick straight out. They bend almost to the ground, and they don't resemble wings at all. The Incas probably thought the helicopter was some sort of giant spider."

"A giant spider that could fly?" Larkin asked.

"Yes, or perhaps it wasn't flying when they saw it," Hector replied. "Also, don't forget the other drawing that resembles an astronaut. Its proportions are similar to the statues on Easter Island."

There was a moment of silence, marred only by the sound of the aircraft engine.

"So," Larkin said, "let's see if I understand your theory correctly. The Peruvians sailed to Easter Island, spotted the alien base, hung around to see what was going on, either out of fear or curiosity, then sent a few of their people back to Peru, where they drew what they'd seen on the plain of Nazca. Does that sum it up?"

"Yes, my friend, it does.

"I see," Jonas sighed. "Well, *my* friend, your explanation is probably as good as any of the others I've heard, but I still can't help wondering if these high altitudes haven't deprived your brain cells of too much oxygen."

They both laughed as the plane circled over the plain once more before returning to the airstrip.

CHAPTER VIII

MARITZA

Hector could remember their time together as if it were yesterday. Jonas had become almost a brother to him as they worked together at Huancayo and Pucallpa...

Once the equipment was up and running, there remained the matter of writing the message to be sent. Hector and Jonas thought long and hard about its content. This was vital because once sent it could not be retrieved, and it would take over seventeen years to get a reply.

They were both in agreement that the message should consist of three parts. The first part would deal with establishing communication with the aliens. The second part would identify who we are, although, presumably, the aliens would know this from the direction of the signal. The third part would be most important. It would contain the reason we needed to communicate with them.

Jonas began the process by programming the Telecom computer to convert language into a mathematical model, so that both sides could communicate with each other without learning a new language. The problem was which language to convert.

After careful analysis of all Human languages, past and present, the list was narrowed down to Hindi, Mandarin, Swahili, Arabic, Latin, Spanish and English. Although Hector had an obvious preference for Spanish, it was Jonas who first suggested it. He argued that Spanish would be easier to program because it was a Latin derivative. Its grammar was simpler, and there were fewer exceptions. Furthermore, spelling in Spanish was far more logical than English. Spanish was also spoken throughout much of the western world, as was English.

"Besides," Jonas concluded, "we are surrounded by Spanish speaking people. When in Rome...."

So, Spanish it was. Oddly, Jonas did not speak Spanish. However, Jonas didn't need to speak it. The Telecom *did*, and it already contained all the languages in its memory.

The second part of the message consisted of identifying themselves to the aliens. Hector and Jonas decided that the best way to do this was to transmit the entire human genome to the aliens. Several years ago this would have been impossible, but thanks to recent discoveries, and the development of modern computers, that feat had been accomplished in 2000.

"Undoubtedly, the aliens already have this information stored somewhere in their history files. They probably mapped our genome when they were here," Hector said. "All they will have to do is compare the one they have on file with the one we send. This will confirm our identity."

"Like a giant fingerprint in space," Jonas said.

"Precisely," Hector concurred.

That left the third part.

"Once we've established contact, and identified ourselves, what do we say next?" Jonas asked.

"That, my friend, is the big question."

"In a sense," Jonas replied, "it's as if we are in a confessional, and we're about to spill our guts to God. Forgive me Father, for I have sinned. It has been two thousand years since my last confession."

"Seriously," Hector said, "a prayer might not be a bad idea. We must not forget who we are talking to. This race of beings is thousands of years ahead of us in culture, knowledge and technology. To them we are, perhaps, little more than house pets. On the other hand, if they have molded us in their image, we must have the same potential that they do. If this is true, they can't ignore us."

"Whatever we say has got to be the truth. It must be sincere, and it must be relevant. This is not the time for trivialities," Jonas added.

"Amen."

How does one talk to "God"? This was a very important matter for Hector--not just because it was the crux of his project, but because Hector was a deeply sensitive and religious man.

Although the work at Pucallpa was exacting, as well as tiring due to time constraints, Jonas still found time to socialize with his new friend, and to spend time with Hector's family and friends. It proved to be a rewarding experience. Jonas kept a diary, perhaps an old habit acquired from years of doing research work on his computers. In it he recorded the days he had spent visiting with Hector, his young wife Maritza, their infant son, Juan, and the other members of both their families. Jonas also called home frequently to keep Patty and his children informed on the project, as well as to find out how things were doing in Spring Valley. Years later, Matthew would publish his father's diary, and it would become a best seller.

Jonas learned that like most Peruvians, Hector had been raised as a Roman Catholic, and had even served as an altar boy at his parish church. His brilliance became apparent at an early age, and it was through the efforts of his parish priest, Father Miguel, that Hector began his studies.

About twenty-one miles north of Huancayo liesthe monastery of Santa Rosa de Ocopa. Founded in the seventeenth century by Franciscan monks, who established missions in the jungle to the east, its library contained more than 25,000 volumes. Many of these tomes were very old and priceless.

When it became apparent that Hector possessed immense talent in studying and translating language he was granted access to the entire library. It was here that Hector began his life's work. By combining the ancient texts with his own research into the history of the Incas, Hector drew his absolute conclusion that man was not alone in the universe.

However, Hector had not abandoned his Christian beliefs. Rather, he had modified them to fit his scientific model. If, as Hector theorized, mankind's development on Earth was orchestrated by extraterrestrial beings, one was still left with an inescapable question of who created the aliens?

It was Hector's belief that just as God probably used evolution as a tool to create the wide diversity of life on earth, He also used other beings He had created to bring their talents here as well. In other words, the spreading of intelligent life throughout the universe was part of a divine plan. And, what better way was there for God to accomplish this than to have the more advanced cultures "go forth and multiply" on distant worlds.

"Isn't it logical to assume," Hector said, "that at some time in the future, man will go forth and colonize other worlds? What if he finds intelligent life on another planet, but only a very primitive form? Won't man want to study this culture and perhaps improve it, if he can? That is our nature. We humans can never just leave things alone."

And so it was with Hector. Rather than refute God's existence. Hector hoped that by finding other civilizations in space, he might be able to confirm it.

"If they are out there, and I am convinced they are, then they must also believe, as we do, in a divine origin. As I once deduced in philosophy class, Jonas, God can't *not* exist! He's here, my friend—and, as these silent monuments testify, so are they—through Him."

Hector *believed* this, and he practiced his belief with all the devotion that one might expect from a person of faith. What's more, his family supported his belief. This did not mean that there was a cult mentality at work here. Rather, there was a feeling that Hector was doing God's work in his own way, and there was nothing wrong with this.

Maritza also came from a scientific background. A native of Colombia, she met Hector at a seminar in graduate school. Maritza was majoring in bioengineering and agriculture at The Ohio State University, with the hope that when she returned to her home country she might be able to teach farmers to grow crops that would produce products other than coffee and drugs.

Maritza was a slight woman, about five feet, six inches tall, with dark complexion, brown eyes and long jet-black hair. By far her most striking feature was her smile. She always had one, and her optimism was infectious. While studying in America, she had picked up American English with a vengeance, including all the idioms.

"It was not love at first sight," she told Jonas one day. "I mean, he was good looking enough, you understand—but such a brain. All he'd ever talk about was philosophy and science. These are not what agirl wants to hear on the first date. But, once I got him to slow down and relax a little, he came around."

They dated for about six months before Hector finally popped the question, and it was the way he did it, that won Maritza over.

It was a warm early evening in June, 2000, when Hector asked Maritza out on a date. There was nothing unusual about this except that instead of using a car or one of the Jeeps he used in his excavations, the date included a helicopter ride and a blindfold. Upon landing, Maritza was led on a hike into a dense rainforest.

Spotlights shone down upon a new excavation site, and as they approached she was nearly blinded by the reflection of the light off of what appeared to be a gold-plated door mounted in a stone wall! The undergrowth had been cleared away, and it appeared that workers were about to open it. She could also see several officials of the Peruvian government on hand, as well as Hector's parents, Father Miguel, and Maritza's family, too.

Taking her hand, Hector and Maritza walked slowly up to the door.

"I wanted my future bride to see this," Hector said softly, as he kissed her. With that, the door swung open. Before them, in all its splendor, lay the lost city of gold, El Dorado. Several small pyramids, nearly completely hidden by jungle, had been uncovered. Their tops, gold covered, reflected in the light. Several smaller buildings, in which countless gold and jewel-covered idols and artifacts were stored, lay between the temples. More a treasury than a city, its access most certainly would have been limited to the highest officials and priests in the Inca Empire. It was from here that the "highest" offerings would have been made to the gods, and, tragically, the most important sacrifices, as well. "We think even the younger children of the emperors themselves might have been offered," Hector said later. "Some of the burial chambers contain royal appointments, and the bodies within bear all the markings of human sacrifice." A last, desperate attempt by the Incas to contact their gods.

It was a monumental discovery, and with it, Hector's future was assured. Father Miguel performed the ceremony in the chapel at Santa Rosa. Ten months later, Juan Hector Villa-Ramos made his first appearance as the son of Hector and Maritza. It seemed like only yesterday.

CHAPTER IX

FINAL PREPARATIONS

In the final hours before the start of transmission at midnight on June 19, 2002, Jonas and Hector worked at a feverish pace. All lay in readiness for the big moment. The programs were loaded. The back-up programs were loaded and the messages were encrypted. The transmission equipment was in stand-by and the laser was set. Connection with the orbiting communications satellite was established. The power generators, and the back-up power generators were on-line and in standby-by modes respectively. The air conditioning units were humming and their back-up units were in stand-by as well.

The message, in three parts, would be started at exactly one second after midnight on June 19 and continue until completed at twelve midnight on June 20, exactly twenty-four hours in length to the second.

The first part, establishing a common language, was allocated four hours. During this period, Spanish, the chosen language would be reduced to mathematical symbols. Spanish grammar would be reduced to equations and every word in the Spanish vocabulary would be assigned a numerical value. Once this was done, the entire package would be transmitted. When, or if, a response was received, the computer would reconfigure the transmission into Spanish, which could then be translated into any language on Earth. It was also agreed that once the mathematical package was transmitted, an example would be needed to show how the system operated. Therefore, both Jonas and Hector decided that the Holy Bible would be transmitted in mathematical code, as well. Father Miguel would be asked to give a short blessing at the beginning of its transmission.

The second part, which consisted of transmitting the complete human genome, was allotted twelve hours. Once they had established communication, the second thing to do was to identify themselves to the listeners. The human genome is unique. It could be likened to a fingerprint for the entire human race. Assuming the aliens were as advanced as Jonas and Hector believed, they not only would recognize it, they would realize it as some of their own, perhaps best, work.

The third and last part of the message would be the most sensitive. It was allotted the remaining eight hours. Jonas likened it to a TV mini-series. How did one compress the entire history of the human race into six hours?

As always, Hector had an answer.

"Photographs," he said, matter-of-factly. "We'll bombard them with a complete photographic history of the human race starting with the time of their own visit here, and leading right up to the present. After all, a photograph *is* worth a thousand words."

"Not when it comes to storage capacity on computers, Hector," Jonas shot back.

"I know, but it's the most effective way we can get our message across. I've got some friends at U.C.L.A., Jonas. We can put together a video presentation that will, how do they say it, 'knock their socks off'."

And so he did. By splicing together old news footage, copies of historic photographs, and recent videos, a four-hour video presentation was edited to fit the message Hector wanted to convey. It focused on the achievements of man, not just in science, but in the arts as well. It also told of, warts and all, the stories of man's inhumanity. The four horsemen of the apocalypse would be well represented. A Photo Album of Man, as Jonas called it, would be followed, in the remaining two hours, with personal messages.

Hector wanted Maritza to speak, and he also invited Father Miguel to say some words. Jonas, although he still had doubts, decided that he would contribute as well. Each of the students, who worked on the project was also given the opportunity to express their feelings in short segments, which would be edited into the remaining time. It was agreed, however, that Hector's message would be confidential. Only he and, presumably, the recipients would know its content.

Jonas could tell that the form and content of Hector's message troubled him deeply. Knowing Hector, as Jonas did, it was an absolute certainty that this message had to be as perfect as Hector could make it. When the time arrived for Hector to enter his message, All monitors were turned off, and no one was allowed near the area until Hector gave the "all clear."

At 6 PM, six hours before transmission began a large reception was held outside the control room. Everyone who had helped with the project was invited for a final get-together. Maritza had planned this for weeks. "Regardless of how things turn out," she said, "I think we need a party to celebrate all the hard work we've done."

The first thing Maritza planned was the menu. An expert on Peruvian cuisine, Maritza learned much of it from her parents, Luis and Margarita, who owned a restaurant and catering service called the *Machu Picchu* in Lima. Firmly believing in variety, Maritza planned a seven-course dinner, with at least two Selections for each course.

The first course featured *sopas*, or soups. Maritza chose *sancocho de carne* (brisket of beef with noodles and vegetables), and *sopa de camarones* – *chupe* (shrimp chowder with cheese, herbs and spices). The second course, *ensalada* (salad) offered a choice of either *ensalada de tomate* (tomato salad with marinated Spanish onions), or *ensalada limena* (avocado, tomato, cucumber and lettuce). For *entradas* (appetizers), there was a choice of *calamares fritos* (deep fried squid with lettuce, onion and tomato), *choros a la chalaca* (steamed mussels with lemon juice and herbs), *anticuchos* (barbecued beef heart kabobs), and *chicharon de chancho* (deep fried pork with onions and tomatoes). There were four main courses to choose from. The first was called *bistek a la pobre* (grilled steak with fried eggs, rice and potatoes). The second, *lomo salvaje*, was a sauteed mixture of beef, peppers, onions and fries with garlic bread, eggs and fried plantains. *Arroz con pollo* (chicken with coriander and saffron rice) was the third choice, and *pescado frito entero* (pan-fried whole red snapper with rice and salad) was the fourth.

For those who desired only a main dish, there was *cebiche*, which consisted of meat or fish, marinated in acidic fruits, such as *churuba, camu-camu* and passion fruit. It was then prepared with red onions, hot peppers, garlic and lettuce. For Andean tastes, boiled sweet potatoes and corn on the cob were added. Last, but not least, came an assortment of *postres* (desserts), including *picarones* (Peruvian donuts), *churros* (Peruvian style sweet pastry), *torte de queso con fresas* (strawberry cheesecake), *helados* (ice cream), and *ensiled de fruta* (fruit salad

Drinks included soft drinks and juices for children (and mixers), an assortment of imported and domestic wines, as well as *cervesa* (beer), including Peruvian, Mexican and European varieties. Of course, no Peruvian party would be complete without *pisco. Pisco*, made from grapes, which were introduced during the XVI Century, is stored as grape alcohol in half-buried, large, conical, baked mud receptacles. Distilled from must, *pisco* is used to make *pisco sour*, a Peruvian cocktail known throughout the world. The cocktail is made from *pisco*, egg whites, sugar, lemon juice, syrup, Angostura bitters, ground cinnamon and crushed ice.

Maritza also knew that good music would be essential and she chose only the best. Back in 1984, a young quartet was just getting started. Using authentic Andean instruments, they played traditional Peruvian and contemporary music in small clubs and restaurants in Lima. Among these was the *Machu Picchu*. Now, nearly twenty years later, *WAYANAY INKA* was one of the most popular acts in Peru, with a world wide following. Their many best-selling albums featured such songs as "Flight of the Condor," "Caroling Donkees," and classical pieces such as "Minuet of Bach."

Andean instruments produce unique sounds. The wind instruments are varieties of flutes, such as the *rondador* and the *ocarina*. Percussion instruments are made from hollowed tree trunks (*bombo*), dried cacti (rainsticks), or goat-skin (*wankara*). String instruments consist of guitar (*charango*), or *kirkincho* (*charango* made with armadillo shell). In addition to native instruments, the group also used violin, harp and European guitar to bring new styles and rhythms to Andean music.

After dinner, which all agreed was a rousing success, there was dancing. Maritza and Hector even got into *La Marinera*. This *mestizo* dance is intended as a dance of courtship, of love, where the man keeps insisting despite his partner's coquettish feminine wiles. Elegant and complex, it is one of those rare dances where the woman marks the rhythm and leads her partner. WAYANAY INKA supplied the music, with Spanish guitar, a Creole box, and the African jawbone of an ass!

Following the dancing, it was time for speechmaking and toasting. Hector thanked everyone for their work, and gave a brief synopsis of the chain of events leading up to this moment. "I particularly want to thank my good friend, Jonas Larkin for leaving his family and his work to come down to this god-forsaken hell-hole in order to make the project successful. Jonas, if you'd be so kind as to stand up, I'd like to propose a toast."

As Jonas stood, everyone picked up his or her glass. "To Jonas!" Hector shouted. "To Jonas!" they all replied. Then Hector said, "Jonas, my friend, we have a special surprise for you."

Taking Jonas into the control room, Hector switched on the big monitor. There, in nearly full size, were Patty, Holly and Matthew. By special Internet hook-up, Jonas was able to speak with and to be seen by his family back home.

"Hi Dad! Hi Hector!" they shouted.

"Hello," Hector replied. Jonas was too busy admiring his family to speak. "If you don't mind," Hector said, "I think I'll rejoin the party. It was nice meeting you."

"It was nice meeting you, too," Patty replied.

Hector quickly and quietly left the room. Jonas continued to stare at his wife and children.

"Well, Honey, aren't you going to say anything?" Patty asked.

"Only this," Jonas replied. "I didn't know how much I missed you all until now."

"We miss you, too, Dad." His beautiful daughter moved her long brown hair from in front of her blue eyes.

"We were going to come down for the party," Patty said, "but Hector said you'd be home soon, anyway, once the transmission is completed. He suggested that this might be more of a surprise. Can you see us clearly, honey?"

"Yes, I can see you all," Jonas said, still staring at his beautiful wife.

"When *do* you think you'll be home, Dad?" Matt asked.

"I think I should be wrapped up here in about three weeks—maybe sooner. Peru owns all this equipment now, so there's nothing to pack up—just my notes and personal stuff.

"Do you think it was worth it?" Holly always came straight to the point.

"Whatever happens," Jonas replied, "it was worth it. I'll tell you all about it when I get home. God, you all look so beautiful."

"You look well, yourself, honey," Patty said. "That climate must agree with you."

"Hardly," Jonas shot back. "If it isn't the altitude it's the humidity. If it isn't the cold it's the heat. If it isn't the smell it's the bugs. I tell you, if it weren't for Maritza's cooking, I'd be a goner."

"Well, you'll be home soon, and you won't even have to miss Maritza's food. She's been e-mailing all sorts of recipes."

"That's great, honey," Jonas replied. "How are you kids doing?"

"Well, Dad," Holly had to answer first. "We really miss you at work. We're starting to do some further modifications and improvements on the 770, but I can't discuss it here."

"I understand, punkin. You can fill me in when I get back. And, how about you, Matt?"

"Work's going well, Dad. I'm still freelancing, but Hal Roberts—he's the editor at Time Magazine—he likes my work. I'm hoping he can get me in there," Matt replied.

"Let me know if there's anything I can do—any phone calls I can make...."

"I will, Dad."

"Well, guys, I guess we better wrap this up. I'll see you all in three weeks. I love you."

"O.K., Dad, we love you, too," Holly replied.

"Take care, Dad," Matt said.

"Come back safely," Patty said. "I love you, too."

"Don't worry, honey, everything will be fine," Jonas replied, as he blew a kiss. "Bye now."

"Goodbye, dear," Patty replied, as the screen went dark.

"Gosh, how those kids have grown," Jonas thought to himself. "Holly in graduate school, and Matty off on his own." It made him think back on his own college days when he graduated *magna cum laude* in physics and math from Kent State University back in August, 1977. He could still remember the photograph. Both his parents were so proud of him, standing there outside Memorial Gymnasium in his cap and gown. His mother, Margaret, stood to the left of him in her pink-flowered dress. A plump, happy woman, Margaret had fine auburn hair, hazel eyes framed in gold-rimmed glasses, and a warm, beautiful smile. To Jonas' left stood his father, Charlie. Charlie was dressed in bright reddish pink bellbottom pants, with white shoes, a wide white belt, a double-breasted checkered sport jacket, and a wide necktie with a red diamond pattern on it. Charlie was a slight man, about five feet nine inches tall (the same as Mom). He wore horn-rimmed glasses over his blue eyes, and his hair was brown. It was the seventies, after all, and Dad wanted to look cool. Margaret had a high school education, but Charlie only made it through the sixth grade. Jonas liked to say back then that his Dad sometimes made Archie Bunker seem like a liberal.

Jonas never forgot the day he brought his father to Kent for a tour of the campus. As they drove around the first thing Dad asked him was why they hadn't torn down "that old shack", which stood on the corner of Rhodes and Summit streets. Jonas tried to explain that the "Partially Buried Woodshed" was actually an artistic creation of the late sculptor, Robert Smithson. All Charlie could say was, "If that is art, then the slums on the East Side of Cleveland must be a masterpiece."

As they walked through the plaza, past the three flagpoles (with no flags flying), Charlie couldn't help noticing the gigantic fountain, which was not working at the time. When Jonas explained what it was, Dad said, "Looks more like the Jolly Green Giant's® Tinker Toy® set to me."

They went into the library. Jonas showed him how modern and spacious it was—the tallest building in Portage County. Charlie looked around and said, "How come the shelves are half-empty? Where's all the books?"

They walked into the Student Center. Jonas pointed out how vast and beautiful it was, with study lounges, offices and game rooms. "What's that?" Dad asked, pointing to the fountain under the grand stairway. "It looks like a public bath. This school sure seems to spend a lot of money on things it doesn't need." They stepped into the cafeteria, got some coffee and sat down.

Jonas showed his Dad a copy of the student newspaper, the *Daily Kent Stater*, to which Jonas occasionally contributed letters and articles. One story talked about possible tuition increases, and another told of proposed faculty cuts. Charlie looked at those, took another look out at the plaza, and said to Jonas,

"You know, son, all the nuts aren't in the trees."

Jonas smiled at his father and said, "And, you know what, Dad, maybe the smartest people aren't in college." Jonas never forgot the look in his father's eyes at that moment. The father and son were equals at last.

Jonas got up from the monitor and decided to return to the party.

Jonas entered just as Hector was introducing his lifelong friend and mentor, Father Miguel. The short (five foot six inches, perhaps), small, dark-skinned priest appeared to be in his seventies. He wore a black tunic, and his cross and beads appeared to be carved from wood—modest, but elegant. He was a scholarly man, with black hair, showing just a hint of gray near the temples. He walked slowly toward the dais, as Hector said, "Father, will you be kind enough to say a few words for us."

Father Miguel paused for a moment, and then he began to speak, "Let us pray. Heavenly Father, in Ecclesiastes we read that there is a right time for everything: a time to be born; a time to die; a time to plant; a time to harvest; a time to kill; a time to heal; a time to destroy; a time to build; a time to cry; a time to laugh; a time to grieve; a time to dance; a time for scattering stones; a time for gathering stones together; a time to embrace; a time to refrain from embracing; a time to find; a time to lose; a time for keeping; a time for throwing away; a time to rend; a time to sew; a time to be quiet; a time to speak; a time for loving; a time for hating; a time for war; a time for peace. Brothers and sisters, may God bless your noble work here, and may Mankind learn the ultimate truth, that God is *the* God of all the universe. Amen."

"Amen."

With these words the party ended as 11 PM was fast approaching. There were the usual hugs, handshakes and thanks, as the guests slowly left. Maritza offered to escort Father Miguel back to his rectory, as Jonas and Hector began final preparations.

The final countdown started at 11 PM. While ever vigilant Jonas looked out for any potential Problems, Hector, about to realize his life's work, was in a state of cautious euphoria. The years of research and endurance were about to pay off, perhaps. But, what if it was all just a pipe dream? Was he prepared for the disappointment that would come 17.12 years down the road if there were no answer? Well, he had 17.12 years to prepare for that eventuality. Right now, he was content to bask in the glow of his achievement. No one could question the quality of his work to this point, even if they disagreed with his conclusion. Science had been well served, and that would be reward enough even if he failed.

"Well, my friend, it has all come down to this," Hector said, as he watched Jonas checking his equipment. "We are either going to send the most important message since God gave the Ten Commandments to Moses, or we are going to go down in history as two of the biggest crackpots in the history of academia. Are you ready?"

"I'm ready, friend," Jonas replied, "but I want you to know that no matter how this turns out, it's been one hell of a ride. Thanks for inviting me."

"Save your thanks for when we get an answer."

"O.K."

The final thirty seconds before transmission seemed to last for an eternity, but as they counted those final ten, nine, eight, seven, six, five, four, three, two, one, the computer switched on, the transmission began, communication kicked in and the laser began sending, just like a well-orchestrated symphony.

Jonas beamed as the process unfolded. For the next nearly twenty-four hours the human race would identify itself, catalog its achievements and deliver a personal message to someone out there. Someone who had cared enough thousands of years ago to come here and to make us what we are. Hopefully, someone who cared still. Mesmerized by the lights and the humming of the equipment, Jonas thought back on several of the projects he and Hector had worked on leading to this moment.

First there had been the new Hayden Planetarium in New York.

Built where the old Hayden had stood, at Central Park West and 81st Street, the Rose Center for Earth and Space was unlike any other structure in the world. Literally, a sphere inside a crystal cube, the building was as functional as it was beautiful. The Great Sphere was really two hemispheres attached at the equator. The top half was a Space Theatre, where a spectacular virtual universe was created using the most sophisticated technology available. Jonas had worked on it. This theatre could re-create the galaxy using actual astronomical data from NASA, as well as the European Space Agency's Hipparcos database of more than 100,000 nearby stars. Jonas had worked on the statistical database of more than two billion stars, developed by the museum, to complete a model of the entire Milky Way Galaxy!

The lower half of the Great Sphere contained Big Bang Theatre, which Hector had helped to develop. Here the first moments of the universe were re-created. This was followed by an awe-inspiring journey, which chronicled the evolution of the universe through thirteen billion years of history on a scale where the thickness of a human hair would equal 30,000 years or about the length of Man's existence on Earth! How ironic it was that both Hector and Jonas had been present for the grand opening in February, 2000, but had never met each other. It was only during their meeting at Telecom that Jonas and Hector discovered they had been working on different aspects of the same project.

Once the planetarium was up and running, and Hector and Jonas had finally met, they were asked to contribute time and work on the "Orion Nebula Project." This involved the San Diego Supercomputer Center, which Jonas had helped to design, and the Hayden Planetarium. The Orion Nebula, which could be seen as a fuzzy patch inside the constellation Orion, is an enormous cloud of dust and gas measuring several light-years across, and is 1500 light-years from Earth. The idea was to create a virtual reality, 3-D computer model of the nebula for projection in the Space Theatre at Hayden. This would enable one to "fly" in and around the nebula, seeing it from different vantage points from onboard a virtual spacecraft. The results were so lifelike that one had the impression of literally traveling at warp-speed through and around the actual nebula. Captain Kirk would have been impressed.

The third, and perhaps most important, project Hector and Jonas had collaborated on involved an actual space mission. Called, simply the MAP Mission, MAP stood for "Microwave Anisotropy Probe" and the plan was to launch a vehicle into space, which would probe the conditions in the early days of the universe by measuring present properties of the cosmic microwave background radiation over the full sky.

This was accomplished, as Hector tried to explain to some of his students, by using passively cooled differential microwave radiometers with dual Gregorian 1.4x1.6 meter primary reflectors. "to provide the desired angular resolution."

"In other words," said Jonas, interrupting, "imagine the universe is a pot roast. We're sticking a sensor inside to see how well cooked it is."

"You have a way with words, my friend," Hector laughed. "Anyway, in April, 2001, the MAP Probe was launched into space by a Med-Lite Delta II 7425-10 missile and placed in a lunar assisted trajectory to the Sun-Earth L2 libration point. This provided for a very stable thermal environment since the Sun, Earth and Moon were always behind the instrument's field of view. The total payload mass was about 800 kilograms, and the mission was designed to last 27 months."

"O.K. So we got it up there!" Jonas jokingly interrupted again. "Now, tell them why, and try to keep it in simple English."

"All right, suppose you have two pieces of wood and you'd like to know whether or not one piece is longer than the other. There are two ways to do it. You can either measure both pieces with a ruler, or you can put the two pieces directly next to each other and see which is longer. With the second method you won't know how long the pieces actually are, only which piece is longer than the other. MAP works the same way. We aren't measuring absolute temperatures, only the differences in temperatures between two points—which point is warmer than the other. Is *that* clear enough, Jonas?"

"Go on, you're getting there," Jonas said with a smirk.

"Thank you, now as to the reason for this project. MAP measures small fluctuations in the temperature of cosmic microwave background radiation. In order to do this the instrument has five frequency bands from 22 to 90 Gigahertz to facilitate separation of galactic foreground signals from the cosmic background radiation."

"You're losing them again."

"I suppose you can do better," Hector said.

"Well, let's see if I can't sum it up. These temperature fluctuations are extremely minute: one part of the sky has a temperature of 2.7281 Kelvin (That's degrees above absolute zero.), while another part has a temperature of 2.7279 Kelvin if I'm not mistaken. Now NASA's Cosmic Background Explorer (COBE) satellite first detected these tiny fluctuations on a large scale. MAP, on the other hand, will measure anisotropy, or temperature changes, with much higher resolution and sensitivity than COBE did.

"Fine," Hector said, "but you still haven't said why."

"O.K. With these measurements, we hope to answer some of the mysteries of the universe, such as its size, its matter content, its age, its geometry and even its fate. We also hope to reveal the primordial structure that grew to form galaxies, and we will also test ideas about the origins of these primordial structures. How's that?"

"In other words, children," Hector said, "we want to know how the universe got here, and this is one way to do it."

As the transmission progressed, Jonas and Hector were both pleased with the way things ran. At one point, a temperature sensor alarm indicated that an air conditioning unit was failing. A back-up unit kicked in automatically to maintain the temperature if the main unit failed. The temperature in the computer room did not fluctuate at all during the process.

Jonas and Hector decided to take four-hour shifts just like navy watches. Hector took the first, from midnight to four AM.

Jonas tried to sleep, but the excitement was too much for him. Perhaps, he thought, a walk would take his mind off things. At first, the humid, tropical air was almost a relief from the canned air conditioning of the computer room. The starlit sky beckoned him. Jonas could see Orion above, with his belt pointing toward a bright, twinkling Sirius. "I wonder if anyone really *is* listening?" he thought.

Staring at the stars Jonas recalled a time long ago, when, as a young Navy petty officer he would walk the deck at night and gaze into the heavens. How insignificant man seemed when compared to the vastness of space. Yet, at the same time, there was something comforting and reassuring about it as well—a feeling that no matter how big and important one's problems seemed to be, they were small in the vast scheme of things.

Jonas was suddenly struck by a foul-smelling stench, which snapped him to attention. "Kin Ville!" he shouted to himself.

It was a smell he had never forgotten. The open sewers of Pucallpa were bringing back memories of another time long ago—a time of sorrow and of lost innocence.

Sitting down on a large stone, part of an ancient wall built by the Incas centuries before, Jonas could see the lights of Pucallpa, but it wasn't Pucallpa he was thinking of. It was of that other place, so long ago.

CHAPTER X

A WINDOW ON THE WORLD

Little Bo Peep has lost her sheep
And doesn't know where to find them.

1971. Another Monday morning on beautiful Okinawa. The weekend over, and with its passing came the endless line.

"O.K., Marine, whip her out," Jonas would say sarcastically.

He was too busy to notice their faces. Men in drab green suits. Some like boys—eighteen, or even younger if the recruiter didn't bother to check. It wasn't his fault. He had a quota to fill—strictly business. Then there were the older ones—sergeants, staffs and gunnies. At least they weren't hypocrites like the officers, those first and second lieutenants. *They* wanted private appointments. *They* were too good to wait in line like the rest, even though everyone in camp knew what they had—the same thing. Even the doctor's got it, but they didn't have to put it in their health records.

"Come on, milk her down." While the guy behind him looked on, the young Marine stroked his penis, pinching off at the base with his thumb and forefinger, gradually working toward the head. If he had it, out came the pale white ooze. Sometimes it was thick and yellow, at other times, runny and almost clear. It had the musty odor of semen, but there was more to it than just dead sperm. A drop or two on a glass microscope slide was sufficient for the test, but sometimes, in severe cases, the Marine didn't have to stroke. He could just let it drip over a waste can, as Jonas caught a few drops.

Occasionally, in stubborn cases, where stroking wouldn't produce fluid, a little prodding was necessary. Jonas didn't have the appropriate wire loop, so he had to improvise. Taking the wooden end of a sterile, cotton-tipped applicator, Jonas would ram it about a quarter to a half-inch into the penis. Then he would turn it a couple of times and pull it out. The slime on the sides of the stick would be spread on the slide, and that would be used as the specimen. If the inflammation was severe, this technique was very painful.

"That's what they get for parking their rigs in the wrong docks," another corpsman told Jonas one day. But, Marines didn't mind pain. "Pain is good," one old leatherneck staff sergeant told Jonas after going through the procedure. "It cost me five bucks, but she was real nice. Fix me up, doc, so I can keep on truckin'."

After passing the slide through a flame to dry the smear Jonas would stain it. He used the Gram method. First, he would cover the slide with crystal violet solution for one minute to color all the bacteria purple. Then Jonas rinsed off the excess crystal violet by passing the slide gently under running water. Next, the slide was flooded with Gram's iodine for one minute. The iodine would fix any Gram-positive (purple-colored) bacteria to the slide. Gram-positive bacteria generally were more susceptible to penicillin. Jonas rinsed off the Gram's iodine gently with cool water and flooded the slide with decolorizer. The decolorizer was 95% alcohol, and if used properly, would remove the color from all

Gram-negative (non-purple) bacteria, but would leave the Gram-positive bacteria purple.

The next step for Jonas was to apply a counter-stain—safranin. Safranin colored all Gram-negative bacteria pink or red. Jonas then set the slide aside to air dry before preparing for microscopic examination.

After drying, Jonas placed a small drop of immersion oil onto the middle of the slide. He mounted the slide on the stage of the microscope and fastened the spring clips, which held the slide in place. By using the coarse adjustment knob, Jonas brought the oil-immersion lens close enough to barely touch the oil, causing it to cover the lens completely. Then he focused in on the field by using the fine adjustment knob.

If all went smoothly, he be looking through a window onto a whole new world. He would see many white blood cells, and perhaps some red blood cells if the infection were severe enough. There would alsobe some cellular debris. If the patient had been masturbating recently, or worse, there would also be deadsperm—maybe a few—maybe hundreds. However, none of this was of immediate concern.

What Jonas was looking for was a particular kind of white blood cell. A white blood cell, containing pairs of little pink or red dots. These dots were infectious bacteria, which had been devoured by the white cells, in the vain hope that this would halt the infection.

Unfortunately, the white blood cells were themselves being digested by the very bacteria they had sought to destroy. These bacteria could not be killed by the body's defenses. If left unchecked, they wouldcontinue to destroy white blood cells, further weakening the body's ability to fight disease. In the meantime, the bacteria would attack the urethral lining, causing burning urination. They might infect the prostate, the bladder and perhaps the kidneys. Eventually they could enter the bloodstream and attack the entire body. Little pairs of pink dots—known in medical circles as Gram-negative dipplococci, or, to be specific, *Neisseria gonorrhoeae*, the causative agent for the most common venereal disease—gonorrhea, or as it was more affectionately called—the *clap*.

And so it went every Monday. Actually, the same thing went on all week, but Mondays were the worst. Around eight o'clock they would begin lining up outside the laboratory door. The higher ranked enlisted men would be at the head of the line, as if this were a privilege. All totaled, there might be 150.

To be sure, they weren't *all* there for gonorrhea. Some were here for syphilis tests. Others had N.S.U. (non-specific urethritis). Still others might have chancroid, prostatitis, venereal warts, and there was the rare case of lymphogranuloma inguinale ("crotch-rot", a viral infection of the lymph nodes in the anus and groin). Many more were here for urinalysis follow-up testing for the gonorrhea they had last week. ("Thank God, AIDS was a *future* menace!" Jonas thought now.)

There were even a few legitimate illnesses to break the monotony, such as flu, hepatitis, appendicitis, gallbladder attacks—and those occasional "accidents". The private who couldn't keep up on the forced march and the gunnery sergeant who kicked him in the stomach. The first lieutenant who blew his brains out with his .45 pistol because his pay roster didn't balance. The corporal who had his first experience with drugs and leaped off the water tower because he thought he could fly. The Marine who tried drilling a hole through a board, across his *lap*—and who suffered a traumatic circumcision. The staff sergeant killed while playing with an "unloaded" gun. "But, hell, doc, we were just foolin' around. We were like—havin' a duel."

Camp Hansen Dispensary, Third Medical Battalion, Third Marine Division, Okinawa, 1971—and just outside the camp, just like a thousand other camps—sat the town. This one was called

Kin Ville. Oh, it could just have easily been Olongapo City, outside Subic Bay, Philippines; or Jacksonville, North Carolina, outside Camp LeJeune. It really didn't matter. The old joke was just as true wherever one went. "If a map of the world were painted on the human body, I know where (Kin Ville) would be."

Kin Ville—Jonas remembered as if it were yesterday—a mixed bag of multi-colored wood and concrete boxes, flashing signs, pawn shops, hash houses, whorehouses, gyp-joints, ear-splitting music, and open sewers. "Binjo ditches" the natives called them. Roadside troughs of garbage and filth, with an odor like rotting vomit, and the narrow, winding, semi-paved alleys that went nowhere in particular, except to the edge of town. There was one main road, however, leading from this town to the next town—the next "camp" town.

The Orimpia was no different from other bars. A Marine walked into a concrete cubicle, which with its dim lights and dank smell resembled a leaky basement. The jukebox was blaring as loud as possible, always with the same old songs. "If you're going to San Francisco, be sure to wear some flowers in your hair."

It took a couple minutes for his eyes to adjust to the light, just long enough for the old man behind the bar, and his wife and the barfly who were playing cards in front of it, to size him up before he could see them.

He walked over to the booth and sat down. There were only two booths, each very small. The tables were only large enough for drinks and an ashtray. The bar was short, with six small stools. An old Kelvinator®, with yellowed enamel, stood behind it. The walls were painted dark green and the floor needed cleaning.

The old man came out from behind the bar, and walked up to his booth. The Marine ordered, "Bourbon and ginger ale." The man went back. There were a lot of fancy bottles on a shelf behind the bar, but they were dusty. What the Marine got came from under the bar, kept in an old "Jack Daniels® bottle, which the old man got refills for from the town bootlegger. He brought the Marine the drink and smiled. His graying hair and gold teeth shone in the dim light. The Marine handed him a dollar. The old man gave back two quarters. Nothing was said. It was understood. "Listen to the rhythm of the falling rain, telling me just what a fool I've been."

She left the bar, and slowly walked over to him. Her age? Fifteen to thirty. It was hard to tell with Orientals. Short, black hair, with rotten teeth. The Marine had seen her type many times before in bars from Nago to Naha. She probably borrowed money from the old man, and now she was indentured to him until she worked it off. It was the same old story in all the other bars, the whorehouses, the restaurants and everything else in town. Her smile seemed to say it all. "I know why you're here. You know why I'm here; so, let's get down to business."

"Quarter for jukebox?" she asked.

The Marine nodded approval.

She took one of the quarters left over from the dollar, and walked over to the jukebox. She knew which songs to pick. That was part of her job. "Michael row the boat ashore, al-le-lu-yah." There wasn't a bad shape to her. She was flat-chested, but most Orientals were. Nice ass, though, the Marine thought as she came back and sat down opposite him. Sipping his drink the Marine thought to himself, This rice bourbon ain't too bad, if you like battery acid.

For a minute there was no sound except the jukebox. "Sister helped to trim the sail, al-le-lu-yah."

"You buy me drink?" she asked.

Again the Marine nodded approval, not taking his eyes off her. She signaled the old man. He brought a glass of Coke®. The Marine took out two more dollars, and the old man gave back two quarters. Nothing was said. It was understood. "River Jordan is chilly and cold, al-le-lu-yah. Chills the body but not the soul, al-le-lu-yah."

He ordered another drink.

"You want dance?" she asked. The Marine knew she didn't really want to, and she was hoping he wouldn't want to, either. However, it was all part of the job, though, to let him think she was only interested in making him happy. She had to keep the jukebox going because she received a two-cent cut on every quarter, the old man got a quarter, and the company kept the rest. "I can't get no satisfaction. I can't get no girl reaction, but I try, and I try...."

A couple M.P.'s walked in, with their neatly pressed khakis and red and gold armbands, carrying billy clubs. They looked around the place, at the Marine—the sucker—sitting in the booth. Tomorrow night it would be their turn. For now there was nothing going on, so they left.

The night continued. The Marine bought drinks. He bought her Cokes®. He plugged the jukebox, and the old songs rattled on. "Round, round, get around, I get around, yeah, round, round, get around...."

There was some dancing a little later, and some jokes. She made fun of his mustache, calling it a "binjo brush." An old mama-san walked in, carrying her tray of trinkets, cheap lighters and watches, as well as a good supply of pornography. She shuffled up to the table, wearing a pair of old sandals. Her gold, rotting teeth revealed in a broad smile, her graying hair combed up in a bun, her short, stocky body clothed in an old housedress with a tattered shawl wrapped around her shoulders. Her appearance disturbed the barfly.Perhaps she knew that the old woman was once a young girl like herself. "Once there were green fields, kissed by the sun. Once there were valleys where rivers used to run."

Such was the fate of the old ones. When they were young, it was easier. The men didn't mind thembeing around. Later, when there were mouths to feed at home, and they weren't pretty anymore, the bars didn't want them, the whorehouses wanted younger girls, and the slop houses already had waitresses. So, they made do as best they could. They bought their weekly supply of junk from the distributor in Koza, and they walked the streets, selling to the drunken servicemen. There were cheap lighters with "Third Mar Div" stamped on them; cheap pocket knives, good for one fight; little stuffed animals for the girl back home; handkerchiefs with palm trees and bathing beauties embroidered on them, together with the inscription, "Okinawa, 1971"; little books filled with dirty jokes; rubbers of various sizes; counterfeit "American" cigarettes; and connections with every "virgin" and pusher in town if the price was right.

At the end of the week, the old women divided the profits with their distributor, got their next consignments, and went home to care for their families. It was not as very pretty life, but, then, nobody asked the Marines to come here.

Nobody asked the sailors to come to Subic Bay, either, to "Pubic" Bay as it was called, or Olongapo City—Where a five-year old could pick pockets faster than a New York pro. Where "Benny boys" (men dressed in drag) would lure unsuspecting servicemen into traps, for robbery, or worse. Olongapo—where women were a commodity, and a man could be stabbed to death if he were foolish enough to wear his wristwatch off-base. Nobody asked the Americans to bring their war machines, their money, or their lust to these little fishing villages. They just came. They asked for what they wanted, and they got it. Democracy in action—free enterprise—the profit motive. That mama-san didn't question things. She survived. The pawn shops, the whorehouses, the bars—they were supplied because the Americans demanded them. It was Economics 101.

So, all right, the Marine was in this bar. He was drunk. The barfly was happy. The old man was happy. The mama-san had just sold him a cheap lighter, just like the one she sold him last night, and she was happy, too. The jukebox was happy. "When I fall in love, it will be forever, or I'll never fall in love." And the jukebox company was happy. The distributor was happy. The military was happy. The whole goddam fucking world was happy!

He got up from the table. His head was reeling. He tried telling himself he wasn't drunk. He tried walking in a straight line, only the trying made the wobble even worse. He stepped out into the street. The air was fresher, but the smell of the binjo ditch was everywhere. He tripped down the street, but his stomach churned. Stumbling into a ditch, the young Marine puked his guts out. A rock band was playing up the street and the bass reverberated in his head. "Love Potion No. 9." He tried to get up. His head pounded. The filth of the sewer and the vomit was running down his jacket—that new one he just bought. The one with the embroidery on the back, which read, "When I die, I know I'll go to Heaven, because I've already been to Hell, Vietnam, 1969-1970, 3rd Mar Div, 2nd Battalion, 4th Marine Regiment." Yes, him, the tough guy, the big war hero. Did he enlist, or did the judge say, "It's either the Marines, or jail"? Look at him. Was he happy, too?

And the glittering lights spun around his head with the ringing bells of the pinball machines, the music, and the noise. He could barely distinguish the men strutting the streets in their finery, looking like cocks in a chicken coop.

He staggered down the street. Perhaps he should have eaten something before he started drinking. Groping along, in search of something he'd never find here, a flashing sign caught his eye. "Honeymoon Hotel" it read. He entered.

A small, dim lobby was bare, save for four old chairs, a worn counter with a lamp on it, which, by glaring at the countertop, partially concealed the old woman's face. The Marine tried to swagger up to the counter, but it was more like a stagger. She was fat, with lots of make-up; red lipstick; and long, red fingernails on soft, stubby fingers. "Five dollar for hour. Twenty dollar for night," she said, before he could even speak. He handed her a five and took a seat along the wall.

Two men were seated opposite him. In the dim light, with his head pounding, it was hard to concentrate on their appearance, but he tried. There was nothing else to do. A black appeared to be wearing green flared trousers; patent leather Gatsby shoes, two-toned brown; pink socks; pink silk shirt with laced front and Spanish sleeves; a green hat with a wide brim and a very prominent feather; dark glasses, and a closely trimmed Afro. Slouched in the chair with his legs outstretched, his head bobbing, he looked to be either asleep, drunk, or more likely, both.

Next to him sat a young white man, a boy really. Probably about nineteen, he had just had a haircut. He was smoking a cigarette, trying to act calm. He had probably been here once before, and he was anxious to get the same girl again. She really showed him something. This young man was wearing brown motorcycle boots, brown plaid flared trousers and a yellow short-sleeved shirt. He also had a poncho-liner jacket heaped to cover his lap.

The old woman behind the counter was the head honcho. She owned the joint, and she "owned" the girls. They each got a commission, probably ten percent of the take, and they were each working off debts to her. Strictly business—the Marine paid his money, masturbated with the bitch, and left. The next Marine stepped up. All-night—every night—there was little emotion and no love involved.

Every week, the old woman took her girls to the clinic to get cervical smears, to make sure they were clean.

As a hospital corpsman, Jonas was occasionally "lucky" enough to be assigned to assist in these procedures. If the girl were clean she could work for another week. If not, she was supposed to stop until the treatment was ended. Many girls didn't wait. Why should they? Gonorrhea produced few symptoms in women. If the

Marines wanted them badly enough, that was their business. As long as the money rolled in, who cared?

A man and a woman came down the stairs. Another satisfied customer was leaving, to go back to his barracks, collapse in his bunk, and dream about his conquest. In another twenty-four to forty-eight hours he would begin to notice the burning sensation when he pissed. The constant discharge would stain his under-wear, as the gonorrhea inflamed his urinary tract.

Then it was back to the dispensary. Stand in line to milk it down. Stand in line to get the green-bordered chit, which said he had "it". Stand in line to have the doctor sign it. Stand in line to receive two 4.5 cc shots of 4.6 million units of procaine penicillin, right in the ass. Stand in line to get his seven day restricted-to-base chit. Stand in line seven days later to have his urinalysis follow-up, which usually confirmed that he *still* had "it". Stand in line to get fifty-six 250-mg tetracycline pills, which came in plastic bottles that said, "Take one pill four times a day for fourteen days." Stand in line fourteen days later for a second urinalysis follow-up. And, if he was lucky, he might be "cured."

So, his restriction would end. He 'd go out in town again. Shack up again. Come back again. And he wasn't alone. Thousands more, just like him, would be doing it all over the world. The *Neisseria gonorrhoeae* would get more resistant to the antibiotics, and stronger dosages would be required. And what would happen if that Marine wasn't completely cured when he got back to the states—to the girl he left behind. The medication might only have masked the symptoms.

Of course, Jonas knew all this. He was a Navy hospital corps-man. He went through sixteen weeks of training at the Hospital Corps School, Great Lakes, Illinois. Jonas worked in that dispen-sary. He prepared those slides. He stood there while those Marines came in, one after the other, unzipping their flies, milking their cranks and dripping onto those slides. Jonas did the studying, and when he was through, Jonas stamped their chits. Sometimes the line got so long he didn't even bother with the crystal violet and the Gram's iodine. He would dry the slide, flood it with safranin and let it go. There wasn't time. Besides, Jonas already knew what they had, and they knew it, too.

So, there Jonas was, walking into that same Honeymoon Hotel, plucking down *his* money, and waiting *his* turn. Well, why not? He was over there for a year. He hadn't ask to come, either, did he?

The black went first, with the same girl who was with the guy who had just left. She shook him awake. She didn't like black men.

Many Orientals didn't. Blacks had a bad reputation There were no black whores on Okinawa unless one was lucky enough to know a girl in the service who was stationed there. There were WAC's (Army) at Fort Buckner, and WAF's (Air Force) at Kadena Air Base. There were a few WAVE's (Navy) stationed at Naha, but there were no Women Marines (commonly referred to as "BAM's", for Broad-assed Marines) at Camp Hansen. Consequently, blacks were forced to settle for the local fare. The Okinawan girls thought they received harsher treatment from blacks., and they also thought black men were more "dirty". Many blacks were not circumcised, and bacteria could thrive under their moist foreskins. Some whorehouses would not cater to blacks at all.

She shook him again.

The black grunted, and looked up at her.

"You come now," she said sternly.

"What's the matter? Ain't I good enough?" Sarcasm dripped from every word.

"You go now, or get out," the old woman said, angrily. "I get M.P. you cause trouble."

"Aw, shut up," he said, slowly getting up. He tried putting his arm around the the girl. She shied away and quickly headed for the stairs.

"Fuckin' bitch," the black muttered, as he followed her up.

The young white boy was getting impatient.

Another man came down the stairs, followed by a girl.

"Nikki!" the boy rose.

"Hi Johnny," she said, smiling. She was a young, petite girl wearing a loose-fitting cotton dress. They often did on busy nights.

The young Marine put his arms around her. They kissed and headed for the stairs. He was happy. She was relieved. It wasn't often she had an easy twenty-dollar job for two nights in a row.

"You *new* here," the old woman said to Jonas. "I got pretty girl for you." She opened the door behind her. There were three girls sitting in a dark room, lit only by a glowing television set.

A girl stood up, still looking at the set. Some kind of Japanese quiz show was on. Slowly coming toward the doorway, she turned and looked at him. She smiled that familiar smile, her long black hair reaching almost to her waist. Jonas gazed at her. Her small petite body was there for him to use, but that was all there was to it—and all there would ever be. Jonas handed the old woman twenty dollars. He took her hand and started for the stairs. Nothing was said. It was understood.

> Little Bo Peep has lost her sheep,
> And doesn't know where to find them.
> Leave them alone, and they'll come home,
> Dragging their tails behind them.

It was funny, Jonas thought, how an old nursery rhyme could take on a whole new meaning, but somehow it seemed appropriate.

Well, this had hardly been the refreshing walk in the moonlight he had wanted, but perhaps it was all for the best. Sometimes we have to re-live painful memories in order to cleanse our souls.

Jonas slowly walked back to the complex, staring up into the heavens. As he approached the building the smell, which had so overwhelmed him, faded as if it were a bad dream. Jonas was able to fall asleep, and only slept fitfully until the start of his watch.

"Good morning, Hector," Jonas seemed to shout, as he came in to relieve Hector at 4 AM.

"Well, good morning to you, too," Hector responded, taken aback somewhat by Jonas' sudden entrance.

"Sorry, Hec," Jonas apologized. "My first break wasn't a very good one, I'm afraid."

"You didn't sleep well? I hope it wasn't the party. Maritza worked so hard on it," Hector said.

"No," Jonas replied, "The party was great—the food—the music—seeing my family—it was all great. I just had a bad dream, I guess."

"You should stay away from the *pisco*, my friend," Hector said, jokingly. "That stuff can kill you."

"I guess you're right," Jonas said, "but it sure was good. Anyway, what's been going on? Anything?"

"No," Hector replied. "Everything's running smoothly. I've just been sitting here, listening to some music. Have you ever heard of a gentleman named Ronan Tynan?"

"The Irish tenor?" Jonas replied.

"The same," Hector said. "Do you know much about him?"

"I've heard him sing on PBS. He's very good, but other than that, no, I don't."

"Well," Hector said, "when Ronan Tynan was 21 both his legs were amputated below the knee. He went on to earn gold medals in track and field. While in medical school (He is sometimes referred to as 'Dr. Courageous'.) he won the 'Marmande' singing competition in France and was invited to be part of the famous Pavarotti School. My point is this, Ronan Tynan represents the 'best' in all of us. I want you to hear something," Hector said as he pushed a button on the console.

There in the computer room, in Pucallpa, Peru, an Irishman began to sing. Jonas had never heard the song before, but the words were very moving:

> "In my memory, I will always see
> The town that I loved so well;

The song continued until the final lines:

> I can only pray for a bright, brand new day
> In the Town I Loved So Well.

"It's a Phil Coulter song about the unrest in Northern Ireland, but it's more than that. It's a song about the human condition. I included it in my message," Hector said, after the song was finished.

"Speaking of messages, Hector, when are you going to share your message with your colleague? Or, do I have to wait for a response, if there is one?"

"Well, Jonas, most of it is personal—sort of like a confession. I'll make you a deal. I won't tell you what's in my message, and you won't have to tell me what's in yours. How's that?"

"Fair enough, I guess," Jonas thought, although he was dying to know. Perhaps some day he'd get a chance. "Would you please play the rest of the album?"

"Of course, my friend."

And there, in the hot and humid Peruvian rainforest, the Three Irish Tenors filled the air with Irish songs—songs of love—songs of war—songs of hope—and of death.

The remaining watches passed uneventfully, and at 12 midnight on June 20, 2002, the message was completed. The programs had run. The computer shut down, and an uneasy silence fell over the room. Hector and Jonas had been waiting two years for this moment, and now it seemed almost anticlimactic.

"Well, that's it," Jonas said softly. "Now, I guess we wait."

"We wait," Hector said, "but first, we toast. I've been saving this," as he reached up into a cupboard for a bottle and two glasses.

"What have you got there, Hector?" Jonas asked.

"Something I developed a taste for back in the States, my friend." And with that he opened the bottle and poured two neat glasses of Johnny Walker Red.

"To success!" Hector said

"To success!" they both toasted, and drained the glasses. Hector threw his glass at the opposite wall, smashing it. Jonas quickly followed.

"What do we do with the rest of the scotch?" Jonas asked.

"Don't worry, my friend, I've a whole cabinet full of glasses—and more scotch as well. We've earned it!

CHAPTER XI

YOU HAVE MAIL

It seems like only yesterday, Hector thought to himself. But, it was seventeen years later, and Jonas was gone.

Hector opened the same cupboard he had opened that night, and took out the Johnny Walker he and Jonas had shared. This time there was only one glass. He slowly poured the dark amber liquid into the glass. The clock above the computer console showed just after 8 PM, July 29, 2019.

"Here's to you, Jonas, wherever you are. We were a great team," Hector said as he drained the glass.

Just then Maritza entered the computer room, along with Juan Hector, now sixteen, and his younger brother, Miguel Jonas Villa-Ramos, named for the two men Hector most admired.

"We thought we'd stop over to see how it's going," Maritza said, as they embraced. "Have you heard anything yet?"

"No, but it's early," Hector responded, as he looked on the faces of his two proud sons. "Actually, I didn't expect an immediate response. They might wait until the message is completely transmitted before acknowledging, or they might take some time to prepare an answer. It could be hours, days or weeks before we hear anything. After all, 7:55 PM was the absolute earliest time any answer could come back."

"Papa," Juan said, "What if there *is* no answer?" Both Maritza and young Miguel were asking the same question with their eyes.

"Well, son," Hector replied, "then we've still learned a lot about ancient mankind, as well as the universe. The time hasn't been wasted. Jonas always said he had doubts about this project, but that didn't stop him from working on it. And, who knows, maybe they just don't *want* to answer. That was always a possibility, too."

"Still," Maritza added, "it would be disappointing, after all this work, not to hear something." Hector nodded.

"Can we stay for a while, Papa?" twelve-year old Miguel asked.

"Yes, my sons, but not too late. Why don't the two of you play one of those games Jonas developed while he was working on the computer? Your mother and I will be next door in the office."

Hector entered the "Games Menu" and told the boys to select one. They selected "Inca", a game Jonas had devised to test motor skills. It involved searching for El Dorado, and was based on some old "Indiana Jones" movies of the 1980's, and Hector's search for the lost treasure.

Hector and Maritza walked into the office, and closed the blinds.

Turning to his wife, Hector said, "There are so many other much more wonderful things we could have done these past years. I hope you're not too disappointed with me."

"I could never be disappointed with you, my love," Maritza said as she turned down the lights. "Does that couch still have the bad spring in it?"

"Yes, but I guess we've gotten used to it by now," Hector smiled.

Back in the computer room, the boys continued playing "Inca". There were ten different levels of ifficulty, and the ultimate goal of the game was to secure the treasure of El Dorado without incurring the wrath of the ancient gods, which guarded the city. Juan had played the game many times, and had managed to reach level ten on several occasions. Miguel, on the other hand, was not so lucky. He had only reached level eight. On each level the gods would place more complex obstacles in the path, and the two boys had to steer their heroes through the various mazes and traps to avoid capture. After about half an hour Juan had reached level four, while Miguel was stuck in level three.

As they played, suddenly the screen went blank.

"Now you've done it!" Miguel cried out. "You broke Papa's computer, Juan. He's gonna kill us."

"I didn't do anything, Miguel. It just stopped. That's all."

"How come it never did that before? You did something to it."

"No I didn't. Wait a minute! It's flashing something. Go get Dad, quick.

Miguel ran to the office and pounded on the door. "Papa! Papa! Come quick! There's something on the computer!"

Inside the office Miguel could hear a sudden rustling. "O.K. son! We'll be right out!"

The office door opened and the two disheveled parents ran over to the computer screen.

Flashing on the screen were the words Hector had been waiting to see for seventeen years:

"INCOMING MESSAGE"

After what seemed like an eternity, but was in fact only about fifteen seconds, the screen went blank again. Then, is bold, stark letters, there appeared a single phrase:

"GENESIS 1:26"

The message stayed on the screen.

What's that, Papa?" Miguel asked.

Hector and Maritza stared at the screen in utter amazement. Finally, Hector responded to his young son. "It's a Bible reference, Miguel. Genesis 1:26. 'And God said, Let us make man in our image, after our likeness: and let them have dominion over the fish of the sea, and over the fowl of the air, and over the cattle, and over all the earth, and over every creeping thing that creepeth upon the earth.'"

They sat in silence still staring at the message on the screen. Suddenly, the phone rang.

"Hello," Hector answered. There was a pause.

"Yes, this is Dr. Villa-Ramos." There was a longer pause.

"Yes, that's right, I'm the one working on the 'Sirius Project.' There was a still longer pause. Maritza could see that Hector was becoming extremely agitated.

"Are you absolutely certain?" Another pause.

"Sweet Mother of God," Hector said softly. This was followed by, "Of course, I'll check my monitor immediately. Thank you for calling."

Hector replaced the receiver. His face was ashen.

What's the matter, Hector?" Maritza asked.

Hector seemed to be staring into space. His mind clearly was elsewhere. Finally, he spoke. "That call," he said, "was from the Mount Pleasant Observatory in Tasmania. We have a satellite hook-up with them."

"Yes?" Maritza asked.

"At precisely 8:30 PM they reported that the Dog Star Sirius suddenly became extremely bright. It appears to be exploding!"

Hector turned on the large monitor located in the computer room. With only a few seconds delay he could see on the monitor the same pictures being observed in Australia. The Mount Pleasant Observatory was located about ten miles east of Hobart, the capital of Tasmania. It was equipped with two antennas, a 26-meter and a 14-meter, which were both prime focus instruments. Since Sirius was much more visible in the Southern Hemisphere, Hector had made arrangements with several observatories including the Observatorio Nacional in Brazil and The Asronomical Observatory Ramon Maria Aller at the University of Santiago, Chile. The Aller facility specialized in double stars, of which Sirius was one. Undoubtedly they had seen the same thing.

Hector, Maritza and the boys stared at the screen. The brightness of Sirius was definitely increasing.

"It appears as if she's developing into a supernova," Hector said at last.

"What's that?" Juan asked.

"Just before a star dies, it becomes extremely bright." Hector answered. "Only...."

"Only what, Papa?" Miguel said.

"Only that Sirius gave no indication that this was about to happen."

"Hector," Maritza said with an agitated voice, "surely you don't think *you* had anything to do with this. It must be a coincidence. After all, your signal couldn't possibly cause a star to explode, could it?"

"Of course not, my love."

"Well, then, since, as you say, it's 8 light years...."

"8.56"

"All right, then, 8.56 light years away. It can't possibly harm us, so why are you worried about it?"

Maritza could see that her argument was having no effect. "Why don't you boys run along to bed, now? Your father and I have work to do."

"Can't we stay longer? I want to see the star blow up." Miguel said, plaintively.

"No." She answered firmly. "Now run along, the two of you. I'll tell you all about it tomorrow."

Both boys hugged their father, although he was not paying attention, and then kissed their mother good night before leaving the room. They knew better than to argue when their father was deep in thought, and he was very much in deep thought now.

"All right, Hector, what's troubling you?" she asked after the boys left.

Hector turned toward his wife. "Maritza, what do you suppose the odds are that of all the stars in the universe, the one star I decide to send a signal to explodes right after I receive an answer?"

"But your signal...."

"It's true, my signal couldn't destroy a star! It couldn't destroy anything! But, what about the beings who received that signal? What about them?"

"Let me understand you. You are saying that the beings you've contacted may be destroying Sirius? But, Why?"

"To demonstrate their power. If they can destroy a star, imagine what they can do to us."

"But, my love, you've said all along that they helped create us. Why would they harm us now? We couldn't possibly pose a threat to them."

"I don't believe that they intend to harm us. However, I *do* believe that this is their way of making a point. There are no planets orbiting Sirius, no life forms to worry about. What's one star, more or less?"

"And you think they have that much power?"

"Why not? If my theory is correct, look how much they *already* had a thousand years ago."

"Well, then, what do *we* do now?" Maritza asked. "All we've got is an exploding star and a Bible citation

"Genesis 1:26" Hector said. "The answer *must* be there. We transmitted for forty-eight hours and all we got back is 'Genesis 1:26'."

"Wait a minute!" Maritza seemed to be having a revelation. "Suppose 'Genesis 1:26' *isn't* the answer. What if it's the *key* to the answer?"

"Of course!" Hector shouted. "Thank God I married a genius. You mean an access code of some kind? Let's try it."

First Hector typed in **"Open File"**. The computer responded with **"Enter File Name: _____."** Hector typed, **"Genesis 1:26"** and pressed "Return".

"File not found," was the computer's response.

Hector tried other combinations. He even tried entering the entire verse. It was no use. In the meantime Maritza kept staring at the exploding star on the monitor. It was getting brighter, and there was a yellowish halo beginning to form around it. "Wow!" was all she could say.

Suddenly, as if struck by a bolt of lightning, she started shouting, "Wow! Wow! Wow! That's it! Wow!"

"Wow what?" Hector hurriedly shouted back.

"The 'Wow' Signal!" Maritza shot back. "When I was at Ohio State we had a series of orientation lectures on the history of the school. One of them was by a Dr. Jerry Ehman. He told us about the Big Ear Radio Observatory that was built in the late fifties and early sixties."

"Yes," Hector said, "I remember it. It was part of the SETI Project, the search for extraterrestrial intelligence. Jonas and I discussed SETI once. Go on."

"He told us how one day he was looking at a printout of signals they'd received and there was one so strong it was off the chart. It had a code, but I can't remember it."

"Don't worry, my dear," Hector said. "It's here." Typing in the key words, **"Big Ear"** on the computer, within seconds Hector and Maritza had a complete history of the project, as well as the signal Maritza remembered.

The initial design for Big Ear was completed in 1955 by Dr. John D. Kraus, professor at Ohio State. A parabola 360 feet long and 70 feet high was constructed on twenty acres of land donated by nearby Ohio Wesleyan University. Most of the work was done by students. By the fall of 1956, the foundation pillars had been poured. In the spring of 1957, the students began assembling the parabola itself. Ninety-six trusses, each 30 feet long and made of steel angle and rod, were assembled in an abandoned factory building, and hauled to the site. By 1958 all bays of the parabola had been assembled and raised, and by the summer of 1959, the foundation had been excavated and the concrete poured for the nine flat reflector bays. During the summer of 1960, the tiltable reflector was completed. (Dr. Kraus got the idea for design of the tiltable apparatus by watching a Ferris wheel turn at a county fair!)

Work then began on the three-acre ground plane between the flat reflector and the parabola. A base of several inches of concrete was covered with aluminum sheeting. Huge machines were brought in to move the 20,000 tons of earth, which had been piled between the reflectors. By July, 1961 the concrete had been poured, and in September work began on laying the aluminum, which came in rolls that were five feet wide and had to be glued down with foul-smelling asphalt-like substance. The work was done in hot, dry weather. The workers were broiled not only by the sun, but also by the reflection off the aluminum. The final components were assembled, including a $6,000 amplifier, and Big Ear began listening in 1963. For the next fourteen years nothing much happened.

Then, on August 15, 1977, a young Jerry Ehman, then a student at Ohio State, was glancing over the day's printouts, as he had done a thousand times before, when suddenly he saw something so astounding that he scribbled "Wow!" next to it. In order to conserve space on the printouts, Ehman and his friend, Bob Dixon used an alphanumeric code. Each successive value of intensity was 10 kHz wide. For intensities of 0 to 9.99, 1 through 9 printed directly, with zero being blank. The value 10 was assigned "A", 11 was "B", etc.

The "Wow!" Signal, which Jerry Ehman saw on his printout was "6EQUJ5". Thus, at it's peak, which would be "U", the "Wow!" Signal was registering at between 30.0 and 30.999... x 10 kHz, the strongest signal ever recorded, and it had not been duplicated since.

"The 'Wow!' Code," Maritza said, looking at her husband.

"All right, so now we have the code. But, dear wife, what does that have to do with this? We're talking about something that happened forty-two years ago."

"Yes, Hector, but think about what was happening then. Man was perfecting telecommunications. Satellites were circling the globe. The first American moon landing was on—when?"

Hector typed in the question and got an immediate answer, **"Apollo 11, July 20, 1969."**

"That's a little over eight years before the 'Wow!' signal. Maybe it was some sort of a test. You know—a test to see how far we'd progressed. Were we advanced enough to receive a signal? It would have to be loud enough for us to hear it, and this one certainly was."

"A possibility, I suppose, but how would they know about Ehman's code?" Hector asked, still not convinced.

"Honey, you said it yourself. We're talking about beings who can blow up stars. A simple alphanumeric code shouldn't be a problem for them, trust me. Type it in. What have we got to lose?" Maritza replied.

Hector shrugged, and typed, **"Open File."** The computer again replied, **"Enter File Name:**

_____." Hector typed, "6EQUJ5" and pressed "Return".

CHAPTER XII

BIRTH AND REBIRTH

Out in the Pacific, night was falling on remote Rapa Nui. The waves washed ashore, as they had been doing for countless thousands of years. The moai, standing in their stony silence, as they had been doing for hundreds of years, stared outward into the starlit sky.

The inhabitants of Easter Island were settling into another evening of peace and quiet, just as their ancestors had been doing for generations.

For young Carlos Sanchez, however, it was the end of an exciting day, because, for the first time he had been helping his father with the birthing of lambs. These new arrivals would join their flock, which grazed the hillsides on the remote island.

Carlos, aged ten, was the fifth generation of his family to raise sheep here. His great-great grandfather, Jesus, landed on Ester Island back in 1890 after crossing by ship from native village of La Calera, via the port of Valparaiso. Chile had annexed Easter Island in 1888, and wanted Chileans to settle the island. Jesus had volunteered. Upon his arrival, Jesus met a young native girl named

Ohomi and started a family. Family legend had it that Jesus was descended from Inca royalty and Spanish conquistadores, but this was a common story among many Chileans.

With his round face, straight black hair and brown eyes, Carlos resembled a brown cherub, always smiling and happy. He was the youngest of four children. His two older brothers, Juan and Pablo, herded sheep like their father, Jose. His sister, Rosalita, worked beside their mother, Corazon, doing the household chores and trying to manage their modest home near Hanga Roa, the only settlement on the island.

The Rapanui people, as residents of the island were called, continued to raise sheep and cattle on the eastern side of the island. Some engaged in fishing, while others, spurred on by the growth of tourism, were employed at the hotels. Rosalita worked as a housekeeper at the Hango Roa Hotel, while Carlos' older brothers held maintenance jobs there, and at the Hotu Matua Hotel, when not tending the herds. It was a good life, if not exciting, and the family was content.

Yes, today was like most other days on the island, except for the birthing of the lambs. This birthing was unusual because it came "out of season." Most sheep bred between August and December. With a gestation time of about four and one-half months, these new lambs must have been conceived in late February or early March. The ewe, Carmelita had never produced lambs so early before, so this was, indeed unusual.

In any event, they were here now, and Carlos had helped his father with the delivery.

"Carlos," Jose said, as they awaited the arrival, "let me show you how to tell when the ewe is ready to give birth."

"Yes, father," Carlos said inquisitively. He listened intently as his father began to explain.

"Well, my son," Carlos began, "if the ewe is giving birth for the first time it sometimes can be difficult to tell. But with

Carmelita here, it is easy. She has given birth three times before, although never this late. The first thing that happens is that her udder fills with colostrum, or 'first milk' shortly before labor begins. That is the milk the newborn lambs will need right after birth to help them grow strong, and to fight disease. Look how large and firm her udder is."

"Yes," Carlos said, almost in amazement as he observed the enormous udder and engorged teats.

"Now," Jose continued, "see her 'dropped' abdomen, and notice that hollow area below her hip bone."

"I see it!" Carlos exclaimed.

"That means she is about ready," Jose said as they continued to watch the ewe.

Presently, Carmelita passed her mucous plug onto the ground. As Carlos watched intently, Carmelita began pawing the ground. As she moved away from the other sheep, Jose urged her from the yard into a straw-covered stall in their small barn. Carmelita began straining and pushing as amniotic fluid was expelled. Jose thought that his young son might become ill at the sight and smell of the birthing process, but Carlos was made of sterner stuff. He watched, almost as if in a trance, as Carmelita was now well into the second stage of delivery. As Carlos observed her strain and grunt for nearly an hour he grew tounderstand why this natural process was called "labor."

Suddenly, Carlos saw two feet emerge from the birth canal. These were quickly followed by a muzzle, struggling for its first breath. Quickly, Jose broke the amniotic sack, and out slipped a wet, black newborn lamb onto the clean, dry bedding.

Carlos fairly beamed at seeing the new life lying on the fresh straw.

Carmelita, however, had one more surprise to deliver.

The second lamb was not so easy. Straining with neither an amniotic sack, nor feet protruding from the vulva, Jose could see that this delivery was going to be a breech, that is, the lamb was reversed from its normal position and its rear was facing the birth canal. As Carlos gaped in awe, his father reached up into the reproductive tract with his right arm. Carmelita's was large and well lubricated due to previous births and the fact that one lamb had already been passed. Trying to identify a lamb's body parts when one's hand is exploring the inside of a ewe's reproductive tract is no easy feat, but Jose had done this many times before.

Grasping the front hooves, Jose turned the lamb, while pulling at the same time. Out popped the second black, wet lamb onto the straw.

The mother, exhausted from the ordeal, now rested beside her new offspring.

Next, Jose showed Carlos how the umbilical cords must be dipped into a strong (7%) iodine solution in order to prevent infection.

After drying off the newborn lambs, Carlos and Jose watched as they each struggled to stand.

"Now, we must wait to see if Carmelita accepts her new lambs," Jose said. "If not, we shall have to bottle-feed them."

Slowly the young lambs stood on their shaky new legs. They both looked healthy enough, the first-born a young ram, the second a ewe. Carmelita was struggling to stand also.

Jose and Carlos watched anxiously for nearly an hour as the two lambs slowly gained strength and approached Carmelita, with her swollen udder, and waiting colostrum. If, after about sixteen hours following birth, the lambs had not ingested the colostrum, they would lose the ability to absorb the mother's antibodies, and bottle-feeding would become necessary. Fortunately, in this case, they need not have worried. Carmelita was a good mother, and readily accepted her young charges.

"Now, my son," Jose said, "we must wait for one more thing. It is called the afterbirth. Carmelita will deliver it. Always let the mother eat it if she wants to. It helps her return to normal size after giving birth. If she doesn't want to eat it, we must throw it away."

"Yes, father," Carlos said, as they continued to look at the two young lambs. Finally, Carlos asked, "Papa, now that I have helped you, can I name the lambs?"

Jose thought for a moment and then said, "Of course,"

"Very well," young Carlos said. Pausing briefly, he announced, "The ram I shall call 'Arturo.' Someday he will win many prizes."

"Arturo it is," said Jose, "and what will you name the ewe, my son?"

"She will be called Rosalita," Carlos answered almost immediately.

"And why would you give the ewe the same name as your sister?" Jose asked, smiling.

"Because Mama always complains that Rosalita does everything backwards," Carlos answered triumphantly, as they both started to laugh.

After Jose returned to the house to tell everyone the good news, Carlos remained behind to observe the new life. The two lambs were suckling now, and Carmelita seemed content with her new motherhood.

Carlos closed the gate to the pen outside the barn and began walking toward the house. As he did so he looked up into the starlit heavens. One star in the southern sky seemed particularly bright tonight, and as Carlos observed it twinkling, the brightness seemed to be intensifying dramatically.

Running into the house, Carlos yelled out, "Papa! Papa! Come quick!"

Thinking something was wrong with the newborn lambs, Jose came running immediately. "What is it?" Jose shouted as he came to the door.

"Up in the sky!" Carlos pointed toward the southern heavens.

As Jose watched, the star grew increasingly bright, and, after a time, it appeared as if a ray of light descended from the star to a location on the ground, some distance away. Jose watched the light with a mixture of curiosity and trepidation. Clearly this was no ordinary occurrence. It must be some sort of optical illusion; yet, there was something oddly familiar about it. A feeling of relief, no, comfort seemed to come over the man as he watched.

Jose smiled, and as he did so, he trembled ever so slightly. Almost as if he were in a hypnotic trance, slowly, softly, the words began to form as he spoke to himself, "...and, lo, the star, which they saw in the east, went before them, till it came and stood over where the young child was. When they saw the star, they rejoiced with exceeding great joy."

"What is it, father?" Carlos asked. "What do you see?"

"Do not worry, my son," Jose replied. "Everything will be all right. Go get your mother, your brothers and your sister, quickly."

"Yes, father." Carlos ran back toward the house.

"And, Carlos!" Jose called, "tell your mother I said to bring along the new lambs."

"Why, Papa?"

"Never mind why, son," Jose said. "Just do it."

"Yes, Papa."

With a feeling of overwhelming serenity, Jose walked toward the light.

* * *

Two hundred thirty-five miles above Rapa Nui, and beyond the bonds and confines of Earth, the International Space Station *Alpha One* orbited the globe in peaceful serenity, as it had been doing ever since the first section, or service module was launched into orbit from Baikonur Cosmodrome, Kazakhstan, back on November 20, 1998.

Upon its completion in 2006, the ISS was the largest and most complex international scientific project in history, combining the scientific and technological resources of sixteen nations, including the United States, Canada, Japan, Russia, eleven member nations of the European Space Agency, and Brazil.

Four times larger than its predecessor, the Russian *Mir* Space Station, *Alpha One* boasted a total mass of 1,040,000 pounds. It measured 356 feet across and 290 feet long, with nearly an acre of solar panels to provide electrical power to six state-of-the-art laboratories. Its overall appearance resembled a fix-winged butterfly gliding above Earth.

By positioning the station at an altitude of 235 statute miles with an inclination of 51.6 degrees *Alpha One* could be reached by launch vehicles from all the partners. This placement also afforded an excellent view of Earth with coverage of eighty-five percent of the globe and over-flight of ninety-five percent of the population.

The space station was constructed over a five year period. It required forty-five assembly missions, of which thirty-six were Space Shuttle flights. This did not include re-supply missions and change outs of Russian Soyuz crew return spacecraft. More than 850 clock hours of space walks, both American and Russian, were required to maintain and to assemble the space station.

For the past fourteen years, the station had been home for rotating crews of from six to seven members, engaged in various research projects. With nearly 46,000 cubic feet of pressurized space, approximately equal to the combined size of two wide-body jumbo jet planes, the station's six laboratories were used for many important research projects.

Protein crystal studies helped scientists better understand the nature of proteins, enzymes, and viruses which led to the development of new drugs and a better understanding of the fundamental building blocks of life. Tissue culture studies helped to test new treatments for cancer without risking harm to patients. Life in low gravity led to a better understanding of the body's systems and similar ailments on Earth, as well as to better preparation for future long-term human exploration of space. The effects of weightlessness on flames, fluids and metals were also studied. Other studies dealt with the nature of space itself, such as vacuum, absolute zero, and, of course, weightlessness.

The space station was an invaluable vehicle for observing the Earth itself. Volcanoes, pollution patterns, oil spills, weather patterns, and studies of large-scale, long-term changes in the environment, and their impact on agriculture, forestry and the oceans were all studied with lasting and beneficial results.

Private business had also profited from the station by conducting experiments, which had led to the development of new products and services for use on Earth, as well as on future space projects.

But that was history.

Now, the space station was largely silent except for a skeleton crew of three who were busy conducting inventory and cataloguing equipment, programs and supplies, which would be transferred to an even larger facility. Soon, like its predecessor *Mir* which ended its life in a fiery burnout over the Pacific on March 23, 2001, *Alpha One* was scheduled for a similar fate within the coming months.

Beginning in 2015, construction began on a new International Space Station, code named *Ark II*, which would dwarf *Alpha One*. When completed in 2021, this station would be nearly four times its size, with a capacity of thirty scientists and crewmen.

In charge of this shutdown operation was thirty-one year old Colonel William "Wild Bill" Whaley of the U.S. Air Force. Second in command was thirty-two year old Colonel Vasily Grinchkov of the Russian Army, and the third member of the team was British civilian astrophysicist Reginald "Reg" Thacker of the Royal

Observatory at Greenwich. Reg was the "old fart" on the team, at age forty-two.

This was Colonel Whaley's third mission to *Alpha One*. On two previous missions he had ferried replacement crews and supplies. He was already assigned to the next mission to *Ark II*, which would carry the computer module for the new station. This latest computer, an updated and expanded version of the old Telecom 770, was currently being assembled by its designer, Holly Larkin, at Kennedy Space Center.

For now, this current mission was two-fold. In addition to the shutdown of *Alpha One*, stored within the cargo bay of Space Shuttle *Destiny*, currently docked with the station was *Deep Space Probe 2*. It was the second in a series of six probes that were being launched to explore nearby stars. *DSP1*, launched nearly a year ago, was headed toward Proxima Centauri, Sun's nearest solar neighbor. Proxima Centauir was a tiny Red Dwarf star, some 4.22 light years away, about one tenth the Sun's mass.

In about an hour, *DSP2* would be detached from *Destiny* to begin its long journey toward another neighboring star. On board the probe were navigational devices, sensors, cameras, transmitters and a computer for analyzing data. The probe was designed to fly by the star and to analyze sensor readings, as well as to photograph any significant objects encountered. All data would be transmitted back to receivers on Earth.

The targeted star for this second mission was to be Sirius, the Dog Star.

Wild Bill had earned his nickname for some of the near reckless maneuvers he had performed as a fighter pilot prior to his entry into the space program. Six-foot two, with straight auburn hair, the native Texan cut quite a figure in uniform, as well as with the ladies. "Howdy!" was his introduction for everyone, and his down home Texas drawl could disarm anyone, especially when combined with his brown bedroom eyes.

Despite Whaley's Texan mannerisms, his laid-back demeanor and his reputation with the ladies, Bill was very proud to be an American, and nowhere was this more evident than when he was working on, or talking about, one of his fondest avocations—genealogy. Roots were extremely important, he thought, because they gave one a feeling of permanence, a sense of belonging in the world. Out in space, looking down on Earth, one could sometimes feel apart from it. For Whaley, ancestry was as much an anchor as it was an outlet.

The Whaley name was an old one, dating back to William The Conqueror and the Battle of Hastings in 1066. It was said that the first person to carry the name, Wyamarus Whaley, accompanied William, then Duke of Normandy, into the battle as his standard bearer. As a reward for his services, Wyamarus was created Lord Whaley of Blackburn, Lancaster in 1067. However, Bill's favorite Whaley was Edward Whaley, known as 'the regicide." Born in 1615, he came from a wealthy and noble family, and was raised to become a merchant in London. Fate had other ideas.

His mother, Frances (Cromwell) Whaley was Oliver Cromwell's aunt. Edward and cousin Oliver were good friends and they shared the same religious views, which placed the liberty of the individual above the tyranny of the crown. When conflict between Parliament and King Charles I boiled over in 1642, both men sided with Parliament and took up arms against the King. By 1649, the King had been arrested and tried for treason while Oliver Cromwell had been given the title of Lord Protector. Wild Bill actually kept a framed copy of the death warrant for Charles I, signed by Oliver and Edward, in his home. He reasoned that it was just the same as someone else having a copy of the Declaration of Independence, because one of their ancestors had signed it. It read as follows:

Death Warrant of Charles the First

"At the High Cort of Justice for the trying and inditing of Charles Stuart King of England January 29th Anno Domini 1649.

"Whereas Charles Stuart King of England is and herewith convicted and attainted and condemned of High Treason and other high crimes and sentence upon Saturday last was pronounced against him by the court to be put to death by a severing of his head from his body, of which sentence execution yet remaineth to be done. Then we therefore do will and require you to see the said sentence executed in the open street below White Hall upon the morrow being the 30th day of this instant month of January between the hours of ten in the morning and five in the afternoon of the same day with full effect and for so doing this shall be your sufficient warrant, and there are to organize all officers and soldiers and others the good people of the Nation of England to be assisting unto you in this service. Given under our hands and seals.

Fifty-seven signatures, in three columns, were affixed to the document. Oliver Cromwell's was second in the left column, and Edward's was third. Edward actually witnessed the execution.

However, unlike the American Revolution, this one ultimately failed. After Cromwell died, the monarchy was restored in 1660. The new King, Charles II swore vengeance upon all those who had slain his father. Many were hunted down and killed. Edward fled to America, where, for the next twenty years, he hid out in homes of friends, or in barns and basements, avoiding the King's agents.

Bill delighted in sharing family stories with Reg, his English captive audience. He even showed Reg a small Whaley family crest, which Bill carried on every mission as a good luck charm.

"I see," Reg said, trying to conceal his boredom with the whole affair, "and you, I take it, are the living proof that the King's agents never found him?"

"Yup!" Bill replied. "I'm his direct descendant."

"How unfortunate," Reg declared. Bill, at first puzzled by the response, suddenly got the joke. They both had a good laugh.

Grinchkov, or "Grinch" as Bill called him, was his exact opposite. Vasily, a stocky man at five-feet eleven, with a crewcut of nearly black hair, was all business. Originally a helicopter pilot who fought against the rebels in Chechnya, he had switched to fighters after the rebellion ended. From fighters he had graduated to astronaut training, where he was assigned to Baikonur in 2016. This was his first mission on board the station. He had previously flown on two re-supply missions from the Cosmodrome.

Dr. Reg Thacker personified the British professor with his "proper" decorum and professionalism. His presence was necessary to assure proper launch of the probe, as well as to aid in the cataloguing of equipment and programs scheduled for transfer. With his gray hair and hazel eyes Reg was the referee between Wild Bill and Grinch.

Life aboard the station varied from dull routine to high anxiety depending on the requirements of the job. Whether it was space walking to repair a sluggish robotic arm, or counting the number of files on the hard drives, there was always something to do. This was especially true when shuttles arrived with supply deliveries. *Destiny* had been docked with *Alpha One* for five days now, and was due to depart in forty-eight hours, after *DSP 2* was launched.

Destiny carried a crew of five, and although the shuttle and space station were conjoined, the two crews were living in two different worlds.

Aboard the shuttle, things worked smoothly for the most part, and when something went wrong, ground support was excellent.

Aboard the space station, struggle was often the norm, and friction between the crew and ground controllers, if not between themselves, was often heated.

For instance, when NASA decided that the crane assembly inside the cargo bay needed adjusting before the launch of *DSP 2*, ground engineers worked on the problem around the clock. When a plan was devised, two astronauts on the ground suited up and hopped into a water tank used to simulate weightlessness. When they were finished testing the plan, NASA ground controllers even told the shuttle astronauts which torque settings to use on their power tools and gauged the degree of difficulty for each task.

"Well, it sounds like you guys thought of everything," said Allison "Ally" Mantell, one of the two spacewalkers who made the repair.

Later, in a television interview, the shuttle crew felt loose enough to horse around a little when Mantell and shuttle commander Brian Forster took perpendicular positions to others in the weightless cabin, as if they were standing on walls.

By contrast, the space station crew was dealing with an air conditioner that broke down several days earlier when the system that removed carbon dioxide from the air also broke down. Since the systems were on the Russian module the international crew of three elected Vasily to deal with Russian ground controllers who scolded him after the astronauts decided to set up an alternate system for removing the potentially dangerous gas. "You could have damaged it," said a ground controller.

"Well, we had to breathe with something!" Vasily shot back.

At one point the exchange became so heated that an American ground controller was heard to say, "Hey, Guys, don't swear at me."

"What do you expect?" Bill complained. "Look, we're trying to fit thirty hours of work into an eighteen-hour day. We haven't been getting the eight hours sleep we're supposed to. And, what about the two hours of exercise? I thought we were supposed to do that in order to 'slow progression of bone loss and other health problems associated with weightlessness,'" Bill concluded, quoting the manual.

Not to be outdone, Vasily had a few choice words for his Russian ground controllers as well. "I've been working thirteen hours without any exercise or anything," Grinch complained, "so don't call me. I'm having lunch!"

Still, work did progress as well as could be expected. Reg was surveying the files on the space station's older Telecom 770 computer—one designed by Holly Larkin's late father, Jonas—to determine which should be saved. It was while doing this that his work was interrupted by Bill.

"Reg," Bill called in his smooth Texas accent, "come here a minute. I want you to take a look at something." Eager for a break in his monotonous routine, Reg joined Bill who was staring out of one of the view ports.

"What is it?" Reg asked.

"I'm not sure," Bill replied, "but see that bright star over there in Canis Major? Isn't that Sirius?"

Reg peered out the port in the direction Bill was pointing to. Surely enough, the star Bill referred to was Sirius, only...

"How come it's so bright? I've never seen a star that bright before," Bill continued.

Reg continued to observe the star. It seemed to be increasing in brightness even as he stared at it. "That must be Sirius," Reg concluded. "It could be going supernova. This will be an incredible sight, what with *DSP2* headed there. Bill, why don't you contact Houston and see what they think? I'm going back to the computer to see what our sensors are picking up."

Reg immediately returned to the computer console. At the very least, he thought to himself, this will add a little excitement to the routine.

Glancing at the screen, Reg was struck by something he hadn't seen before. A new file had suddenly appeared. Reg was certain it wasn't there when Bill called him away. "Vasily!" Reg called to his other crewman.

"What is it, Reg?" Vasily replied.

"Have you been working on the computer files recently?"

"No," Vasily responded. "That's your department. Why do you ask?"

"Well, there is a new file here that wasn't here a few minutes ago. I haven't seen this one before. Bill called me away to look at Sirius..."

"Sirius?" Vasily asked.

"Yes, Sirius," Reg said. "It seems to be getting very bright all of a sudden, and Bill's checking with Houston to see what's going on. Anyway, while I was looking at Sirius, this file must have popped up on the screen."

"So," Vasily shrugged, "you must have overlooked it, somehow. Why don't you open the file and see what's in it while I go check on Sirius?"

"I guess I did," Reg answered hesitantly, as Vasily left to join Bill, "but I don't see how." Reg continued to stare at the screen. "Anyway, as you aptly put it, Vasily, it's my department, so here goes." Reg keyed in the file number "6EQUJ5" and pressed "return."

Immediately the screen went blank, followed by a flash of light. As Reg watched, almost in shock, a series of light patterns of varying intensities began running across the screen in all directions. It was almost hypnotic to watch. Reg tried to stop the program, but the keyboard was frozen. He even tried to turn off the computer, but the power switch would not respond.

"Bill! Vasily! Come Quick!" he called. The always unflappable Englishman was clearly agitated.

Whaley, who was busy trying to contact Houston, was having no luck. All communications had suddenly gone out. The transmitters weren't dead; all systems showed go. It was just as if, all of a sudden, no one back there was listening.

Vasily, entranced by the ever brightening star, was brought back by Reg's call.

"What the hell's going on?" Bill yelled. He and Vasily joined Reg at the computer terminal. "I can't raise Houston," he said. "It's like, you know, the phone's ringing, but nobody's answering."

"Look at the screen," Reg said. "I opened that file—the one I told you I didn't see before—and look what it's doing. I can't seem to stop it. None of the switches work. And, there's another thing..."

"Yes?" Vasily asked.

"At first the screen went blank," Reg continued, "and then there was a flash of light before all this started happening. I could swear..."

"Yes, go on," Vasily said, becoming annoyed.

"I could swear," Reg replied, "that the flash said... it said..."

"Out with it!" Bill shouted. "What did the fucking thing say?"

"I think it said, very quickly, 'Downloading Jonas Larkin,'" Reg replied, not quite believing what he had just said.

On board *Destiny*, until a few minutes ago, everything had been running smoothly. Commander Forster, along with fellow spacewalker, Ally Mantell, had just finished positioning *DSP2* for launch, and the countdown was underway. Now, with less than ten minutes to go, all communication with Houston, as well as with *Alpha One*, had suddenly gone dead. To make matters worse, the computers on board *Destiny* and *DSP2* were frozen, and all sorts of noise patterns were running on them. It looked like multi-colored gibberish to the commander.

As the light patterns shot across the screen, suddenly there was the sound of a warning buzzer. The robotic arm in the cargo bay was now engaged, and was moving—by itself!

Helpless, Commander Forster could only watch as the probe repositioned *DSP2* ever so slightly, and then detached itself from the probe. *DSP2* now floated independently above *Destiny* and totally out of contact.

"Oh, my God!" Forster muttered. "What the hell is going on?"

All the computer screens went blank. There were several seconds of complete silence aboard both *Destiny* and *Alpha One* as crews on both vehicles tried to regain composure.

A sudden flash of light from outside the two craft broke the silence.

Both crews watched in amazement, and somewhat horrified, as the thruster rockets on *DSP2* fired perfectly, sending the probe off into space. Bill Whaley watched from *Alpha One* as the probe flew further and further away—toward the bright light of Sirius.

"Jesus!" Reg broke in.

"What is it now?" Bill shouted. Hadn't they already seen enough?

"I just saw another flash on the screen," said Reg, almost beside himself, "and this time I really saw it."

"O.K." Bill asked, "What did it say *this* time?" as Vasily listened in.

"It said, 'Thanks for the ride… Jonas.'" Reg replied.

With that, the communications systems were suddenly restored, and all computers came back on line. Both crews stood in benumbed silence. The overpowering thought running through everyone's mind had to be, how were they ever going to explain this?

CHAPTER XIII

REUNION

Because of Daylight Savings Time, it was an hour later in Spring Valley.

It being summer, school was not in session so Patty was putting in full-time hours at the antique shop. She had also started an interior design business on the side, specializing in Victorian décor. This occupied her time, and she was as content as one could be under the circumstances.

Jonas had left her quite comfortable. The children were off with families of their own. Holly was working at Telecom. She met her husband there. They had been married for two years now, and Holly was expecting a baby girl in November. Matthew worked as a reporter for Cable News Network and was constantly on the move. Holly lived in Westchester, and weekly get-togethers were no problem. Matthew would visit whenever he was in town, often on very short notice. Indeed, only that afternoon he had called from Kennedy to say he'd be spending the night. It was good to see him again.

Over dinner, which Patty had prepared on short notice, they chatted about Matt's career and how well Holly was progressing at Telecom. Matt wanted to visit his pregnant sister, and after calling her, decided to drive over there after dinner. Patty wanted to join him, but something told her that perhaps her son and daughter should have some quality time together by themselves. So, she was spending the evening alone. Matt could fill her in when he got home.

After clearing the dishes, Patty decided to take a leisurely bath in the master suite. As she headed down the hall past the den, she was suddenly struck by an overwhelming urge to step inside. Since Jonas' passing, the den was rarely used, as Patty had her own office next to the kitchen. She turned on the light. Everything appeared normal. The dark walnut paneling, the bookcases, Jonas' desk, all seemed in order. His computer....

It sat on a desk against the wall, behind Jonas' tall leather desk chair. Patty hadn't used it since her own office was built. Turning it on, she was immediately struck by the message on the monitor. **"You have mail,"** it said. This was odd, she thought, because since Jonas' death, all e-mail accounts had been transferred to her office. She was certain the phone line to this computer had been disconnected.

She hesitated. What if this were one of those e-mail viruses, or some kind of pornographic garbage. The best thing to do was to hit the "delete" key.

Still, that urge, which had induced her to enter the den in the first place was now pressuring her to read the message. Using the mouse, she clicked "Read message." The screen went blank. "Just as I thought," she mumbled.

"Hello honey." A voice came over the computer speakers. Patty reeled around. "It's me, Jonas."

All manner of thoughts instantly raced through Patty's mind. It sounded just like him. This was far worse than any virus or perversion she could think of. The first thing tomorrow, this computer was going out into the trash. How could anyone be so low as to pull a trick like this? It had to be someone at Telecom with a vendetta. Heads were going to roll. Holly would see to that.

"Honey, please believe me, I tell you, I'm Jonas."

"It can't be! You can't be!" she shouted back immediately. "Whoever you are, my daughter knows everything there is to know about computers. She'll track you down, and when she finds you, we'll see to it that you never do this to anybody again!"

"Holly had a very good teacher," the voice said.

"So, you know about my family, as well," Patty shouted. "You've been spying on us, too, I suppose."

"There was no need to, honey...."

"Don't call me 'honey'!"

"All right—Mrs. Larkin—before you shut me off, let's run a little test."

"What do you mean by 'test'?" Patty shot back, still angry.

"Think of one thing that only Jonas could know, something that only you and he shared together. Ask me one question about it, and if I can't answer it, this message will end and I'll never bother you again. Fair enough?"

Patty did not speak immediately. It seemed like a good idea. If this voice was a fraud, it should be easy enough to find out, and Holly could deal with it later.

Somewhat light-headed, Patty sat down in Jonas' cordovan leather chair.

"All right," Patty said, regaining her composure, but still speaking sternly. "Let me think for a minute."

"Take all the time you need."

Patty thought. What was the one thing between them that not even Holly or Matt knew about? Something so intimate that no one could possibly know besides them. Something that Jonas would certainly remember.

Finally, she spoke. "On one of our anniversaries, you secretly arranged, without even letting our children know, to take us someplace special, and while we were there, they had a particular wine, which you raved about. Remember it?"

"Honey, I remember it like it was yesterday," the voice answered, almost immediately. "It was our fifteenth wedding anniversary. I secretly arranged to have us flown to Mallorca on the corporate jet. We packed Holly and Matt off to summer camp. You and I stayed in a little seaside village on the West Coast, called St. Elmo. There was a villa there called La Torre, and our room was in the tower. The wine was a local red one, with a yellow label. In red across the top it said 'Binissalem', with a picture of a vineyard below. Beneath the picture, in black script, was 'Jose L. Ferrer' It reminded us both of the actor, remember? And printed underneath were the words 'VINO TINTO DE CRIANZA'. I liked it so much I went to the store and bought every bottle they had. I also remember the wonderful leg of lamb we had in the restaurant on the second night. And how about the trolley cars in Soller? I even remember the cut you got on your left ankle when you fell on the rocks down by the beach."

Patty sat dumbfounded as tears came to her eyes. "It *is* you," she said finally. "But, how...."

"How, indeed." Jonas said.

* * *

Back in Pucallpa, Hector and Maritza were experiencing a different kind of phenomenon. After hitting the "Enter" key their computer monitor had gone blank again, only to be followed by another Bible entry:

John 14:2-4

As with the first, Hector remembered it:

"'In my Father's house are many mansions; If *it were* not *so* I would have told you. I go to prepare a place for you. And if I go and prepare a place for you, I will come again, and receive you unto myself; that where I am, *there* ye may be also.'"

"What does all this mean, Hector?" Maritza asked.

Before Hector could respond, a familiar voice filled the room.

"Good evening Hector and Maritza. I see you've been catching up on your Bible readings." Jonas' voice was unmistakable.

Hector and Maritza slowly sat down in front of the console.

"Yes it's me," Jonas said. "I see I'm not getting the same reaction from you that I'm getting from Patty."

"You've been in communication with Patty?" Hector asked, still in disbelief.

"Correction old friend, I *am* in communication with Patty, even as we speak. One of the benefits of being where I am now is that one *can* be in two places at once!"

"I don't understand this at all," Maritza exclaimed. "You're dead. Hector and I both attended your funeral."

"I *am* dead," Jonas responded, "in the physical sense. But, as they say, life goes on."

"You say you're communicating with Patty. Can we speak to her?"

"Later, perhaps. Right now it's personal—between us. Speaking of 'personal', Hector, I finally got to see the message you sent 8.56 years ago, and that's partly why I'm here."

"Where *is* 'here'?" Maritza asked.

"'Here' is wherever I want to be, whenever I want to be there," Jonas replied, "and right now, 'here' is here."

"Are you saying that since your death you have been able to go anywhere at any time you choose?" Hector asked. "How is this possible?"

"You of all people should know, my friend. You believe in God don't you?"

"Of course we do," Maritza interrupted, "but what's that got to do with it?"

"All right," Jonas continued, "then explain how God can be at all places at the same time, and how He has existed for billions of years."

"Because He's God," Maritza said, becoming agitated.

"That's true," Jonas said, "but the reason He can do those things is because He normally exists in a different dimension than we do."

"What are you talking about?" Maritza said.

"I'm talking about God, and one of His finest creations—Einstein. I'm talking about dimensions—height, width, depth and time. Einstein was right about all four. The problem is he left one out."

"Left one out?" Hector said. "What do you mean, Jonas?"

"I mean, Hector, that Einstein only considered the physical universe. He never thought about the non-physical."

"A non-physical universe?" Hector asked, becoming very interested.

"Of course, my friend, the non-physical universe—if God is truly omnipotent then it stands to reason that he can exist in a physical *or* a non-physical state. God is *not* limited by physical laws. Therefore, the non-physical universe is *not* limited by physical laws, either. Time is irrelevant, and travel is limited only by one's imagination."

"This is astounding." Hector said. "Is this what happened to you that day when you had the accident?"

"No." Jonas answered. "I died that day, just as you, and everyone else, will. But, sometimes, after we've crossed into that other place, which you call Heaven or Hell, but which is in fact the non-physical, or spiritual universe, we are allowed to come back. I have been given that chance."

"But, why, Jonas?" Hector asked.

"Because of the message you transmitted, Hector," Jonas replied. "The time has come to tell you what the future holds for mankind, if you are willing to listen and to accept what I am about to say."

Maritza clutched her husband's hands. Hector felt her ice-cold fingers as they looked into each other's eyes. A mixture of emotions swept over them. At once they were experiencing dread and hope, fear and excitement, despair and joy. But, they were both certain of one thing—that overwhelming desire to *know*, which has driven man from the very beginning of time.

"Go on," Hector said.

* * *

"Patty," Jonas said, "I never got to say this to you before the accident, but now that I've been given this chance...."

"What is it, honey?" Patty asked, now convinced that she was speaking with her husband. She could have asked how this was all happening, but it didn't seem to matter.

"I know I could have been a better husband to you, and a better father to Holly and Matt. I just got wrapped up in my work too much at times."

"You were just being yourself, Hon. The kids didn't know you any other way."

"I know that, but when I think of all the times I should have been there for them, like the time Matty broke his ankle at the little league game, or that time I was late for Punkin's piano recital...."

"They understood, Jonas. You explained it to them when you could. It wasn't as if you were ignoring them. You aren't disappointed with how they turned out, are you?" Patty asked.

"Of course not, but...."

"But what, honey? Look, there are no such things as perfect parents. We did the best we could. I know I got testy at times, myself, but we have to look at the end result, and all things considered, it turned out pretty good."

"They *are* pretty good kids, aren't they?"

"Yes, they are, and that's because they had a pretty good father."

"And a husband, Patty? Was I a pretty good husband, too?"

"The best."

"I only wish I could have stayed longer. I had to try it, honey, you understand. I couldn't risk someone else. It seemed safe enough, but there's always a chance...."

"Dear, you have nothing to be sorry for."

"You're sure about that?"

"I'm sure."

"I love you so much. I *know* I never said it enough, but I do."

"I've always known that, dear. Still, it's nice to hear it one more time. I love, you, too."

"Well, I guess that's about all I really wanted to say," Jonas concluded, "but...."

"Yes?"

"Now that you *know* it's really me, doesn't this bother you at all? Don't you want to know how...."

"How you came back? No...not really—just that you did. Are you happy there?

"I am—and someday, it will be even better. But, in the meantime, Patty, make the most of every day. Do good things to others, and good things will come to you. I know that now, more than ever. I—I'm not sure if, or how you're going to tell Holly and Matt about this...."

"I think it will be our little secret, if you don't mind. After all, I can't do good deeds if I'm locked up in a rubber room. Just kidding.

"Perhaps you're right. Well, as they say, 'all good things must come to an end.' I love you, Patty—forever."

"And I love you, too—forever."

The screen went blank. A tear trickled down Patty's face as she slowly got up from Jonas' chair and turned off the computer. Before leaving the den she looked back at Jonas' desk and turned off the lights.

"Yes," she thought, "a nice relaxing bath is just what the doctor ordered."

As she started down the hall to prepare her bath, the words of an old Vera Lynn song from World War II kept running through her mind. She started singing it to herself:

> We'll meet again,
> Don't know where,
> Don't know when,
> But, I know we'll meet again,
> Some sunny day.

CHAPTER XIV

THE SERMON

"Hector," Jonas said, "I think the reason you're hearing this from me is to make it more personal, although I'm not sure I'm the one to say this. Unlike you, I was never very religious. I always figured God's in his heaven. All's right with the world."

"And now?" Hector asked.

"I have experienced nothing less than an epiphany, Hector," Jonas said. "That is the only way I can describe it. I now know that mankind stands on the brink of a new adventure. There are wonders ahead which you can't even imagine. Hector, you were concerned about man's present and his future. You wanted to establish contact in order to help man through his difficulties."

"In a round-about way I guess that's right," Hector responded.

"Hector, the universe is a dynamic environment. The Earth is a dynamic planet, and evolution is a dynamic process. Man may be the ultimate being on Earth today, but what about the future? The power of rational thought is the one feature which sets man apart from all other animals on earth, Hector. This places him above all earthly life forms in being able to control his environment. Wouldn't you agree?"

"Of course," Hector said, with Maritza nodding approval.

"However, it is not incorrect to say that from an evolutionary standpoint, man is the latest in a long line of failures. His ancestors were forced by environmental factors and the law of natural selection to undergo many physical changes. Consider this. Man is a relatively large animal. Yet, for his size, he is a very weak creature. He cannot run very fast. He cannot climb very well. His senses of hearing and smell are not especially acute. Without tools he is a very poor hunter or gatherer. In short, were it not for his brain, man would have been extinct long ago.

"It is evident that in his remote ancestry, only those with the largest brains—the greatest ability to reason—were able to survive, to reproduce and to pass on the gift of free thought. Other animals, possessing superior physical abilities, were able to survive without increased brain capacity. Indeed, it can be argued that the lowly cockroach, by virtue of not having undergone any significant modifications in the past hundred million years, is a more successful animal than man.

"What exactly are you getting at, Jonas?" Hector asked.

"What I'm getting at, Hector, is this, Until now, evolution on earth has been a *passive* process. That is to say, species either adapted, or became extinct. They had no control over their fates. Climatic changes, whether caused by volcanic upheavals, or by meteorite collisions, caused tremendous changes in the flora and fauna throughout the world. There was no alternative. Either adapt, or die. Plagues would wipe out entire species, and there was no way to prevent them other than to become resistant, or to perish."

"Mankind, on the other hand, *does* have control. His evolution is different, in that he can directly alter his environment. He can also directly influence his own development through the use of medicine and science. Man's evolution, therefore, is an *active* process.

"However, as active as it is, it is also unavoidable. Man's insatiable desire to learn, to explore and to change himself and his environment makes his own evolution inevitable.

"Are you saying that man, as we know him, will evolve into some 'higher' form of life?" Maritza asked.

"That is correct," Jonas replied. "However, there is also one thing man must learn first in order to avoid his own extinction.

"And that is?" Hector asked, leaning closer to the monitor.

"Man must learn that *his* evolution is part of the earth's evolution as well. This notion that we must somehow preserve our planet in its present form, while noble in intent, is also misguided. The world is constantly changing, and man's development is *part of* that change. It is not *apart from* it. He must also learn that just as death is a part of life, so also is extinction a part of evolution. Extinction has been occurring ever since life first appeared, and nature cares not whether a species dies because of meteorites, or because of man's modifications of the Earth. The reason is because man, whether he likes it or not, is part of nature. For every species that has become extinct during man's time on Earth, there are many, which have benefited by his existence. And, as man has continued to develop, he has created *new* life forms himself, through genetic modification. He has also become capable of bringing back certain species which have become extinct. 'Jurassic Park' is not as farfetched as it seemed when it was written.

"Of course, it remains to be seen whether or not man, in his latest form, will be able to survive by his own means, or if the forces of nature, or his own mistakes, will put an end to this chain of failures. Recent technological advances are already influencing the outcome. The advent of modern computer technology, combined with human genetic research, is laying the groundwork for future evolutionary changes in the human animal.

"Therefore, in view of the fact that thought is the one distinct advantage we have, it behooves each of us to make the most of this gift and use it to its full advantage. The works of man are all monuments, whether good or bad, of man's ability to think. Thought built the Taj Mahal. It was also thought that built Auschwitz. Thought, then, is a tool. And, as a tool, it is neither good nor evil. It is the user who commits the act.

"The other driving force, Hector and Maritza, is uniqueness. Every person, no matter how trivial or insignificant they may appear to others, is unique. A few—a very few—achieve some notoriety, some form of greatness, which sets them apart from others. They are the ones who either write books or are written about. Indeed, it may be said that being written about is the one and only universal criterion for greatness, because greatness itself takes on many forms. Babe Ruth and Helen Keller were great, but certainly not in the same ways.

"Unfortunately, the vast majority of people are not *great*. No books are written by them, or about them, and so we find the ultimate irony that the vast bulk of human knowledge—of human experience—goes unrecorded, and is lost to future generations. We are left to assume that the thoughts and experiences of the great are also applicable to the not-so-great. Historians like to deal in least common denominators. 'The pharaohs of Egypt built the Great Pyramids.' Of course, they didn't. We know they didn't. Hundreds of thousands of slaves toiled, sweated, starved and died to build them. However, their lives, their experiences are lost. All that remains are giant stone epitaphs. 'Louis XIV built the Palace of Versailles.' He didn't, but it's convenient to think he did—far easier than trying to document the thousands of unimportant laborers and craftsmen, without whom Versailles would not exist.

"Mankind is no greater than the sum of its parts, Hector, and we must never lose sight of that.

"And finally, friends," Jonas said, "don't waste your time looking toward the heavens for a new Messiah. Those ancient civilizations wasted their time and resources doing just that, and where did it get them? In reality, the Messiah is within each one of us. We are all children of our Creators, made in their image. We are each capable of living a just and happy life if only we each develop ourselves to our full potential. There is no need to wait for paradise. It is already here. All that is needed has been provided. The universe is at our feet if only we would realize it. Do not limit yourselves to the petty problems of everyday life, but open your minds to the wonder of the creation all about you. You have eyes. Look! You have ears. Listen!

"Our Creators were not fools, Hector. They did not make time only to have us waste it. They did not give us brains without the freedom to use them. Hell is created when men do not think properly, and, as a result, do not act properly. We, therefore, make our own hells by our incomplete thoughts and improper actions. Thus is Hell created, and thus is Hell maintained.

"When Jesus said 'In my Father's house are many mansions,' Hector, he was referring to the universe. Earth was not the only place where life started. When the farmer plants a field of wheat, he does not concern himself with the grain from a single plant. It is the entire crop that matters, my friend.

"So, Jonas," Hector said, "There *are* other planets with life on them."

"Yes," Jonas replied. "There are several hundred within our galaxy alone."

"Then why haven't we been able to establish contact with any of them?" Maritza asked.

"If I may use the analogy of the farmer again," Jonas replied. "When he plants his seeds, he spaces them far enough apart so that, as they grow, each plant does not interfere with the growth of another. In time, perhaps after learning to escape the limits of the physical universe, man will be able to reach out to other worlds. For the present, however, the time is not right. Man has barely explored the limits of his own world, and he certainly hasn't yet learned how to use it wisely.

"That's very true," Maritza agreed. "Perhaps we just aren't ready."

There was a silence in the room. Hector frowned and tapped his fingers on the desk.

"You are disappointed, Hector," Jonas spoke again. "After all this time and effort, you were expecting to learn the secrets of the universe—perhaps to solve all of man's problems by asking someone else for help?"

"I wanted to *know*, Jonas" Hector replied. There was a sense of frustration in his voice, as if he couldn't adjust to or accept the fact that this was the only answer he was likely to get. "I wanted to establish dialog with other, more advanced civilizations, to share knowledge. Instead—instead, I got a sermon."

Jonas replied, "A sermon was good enough for Jesus, my friend. When he spoke on the mount, he was saying what the people needed to hear, not necessarily what they wanted. 'Therefore all things whatsoever ye would that men should do to you, do ye even so to them....'"

"He's right, Hector," Maritza exclaimed. "We have been given a great gift. Don't be disappointed. We have been given the opportunity to talk with Jonas again, and to hear what the aliens have to say through him. This is a message of hope. This is a message of comfort. We *are not* alone. Someone out there *does* care. Don't you see that?"

Hector nodded. "You're right, my love. You are always right. Forgive me, Jonas, I spoke out of ignorance."

"There is nothing to forgive, old friend."

"But, tell me, Jonas," Hector asked, "there *is* one thing I need to know. These Bible quotes we received. Am I to assume that these aliens and the God of Abraham and Jesus are one and the same?"

"Not at all, my friends. You've no doubt heard the phrase, 'The Lord works in mysterious ways His wonders to perform.'"

"Of course we have," Maritza said.

"Our alien ancestors saw the potential for Earth many thousands of years ago. They came, they cultivated, and they left. But, who created them?" Jonas asked. "Who directed them to do what they did for us? No matter how far back one goes in the history of the universe, there always has to be someone 'back there.' We say that the universe began with a Big Bang. Who triggered it? We say that before the Big Bang there was energy. Who made it? Your faith, Hector and Maritza, has not been misplaced. God exists. He exists all around us, and within each of us. We are part of Him, just as the universe is part of Him. God *is*, and that's really all that can be said.

"Live well, my friends. We shall see each other again. For now, share this message with all of Mankind. Remember what has been said, you have all the tools within you, and in the universe around you. Use them well. Use them wisely. Good-bye for now."

The screen went blank.

Maritza and Hector stared at the blank screen in stunned silence. Finally, Maritza spoke, "I hope you recorded all this," she said. After another brief period of silence, she added, "I wonder what he meant when he said 'Good-bye for now.' Do you think he'll come back some day?"

"I don't know," Hector answered, "but I guess that all depends on us, on how well we listen *this* time. I have recorded the message. Now we must see that it reaches all mankind."

"In a way," Maritza added, "Jonas didn't say anything that hasn't been said before."

"No," Hector said, "but perhaps that's the point, my love. We *need* that reassurance again."

Maritza looked at the monitor showing Sirius. "My God!" Maritza cried out. "Look at the star!"

They stared at the giant monitor showing Sirius. "I can't believe it! It's—it's—reversing itself!"

What had been a supernova only minutes ago was turning back into a star, just as it had been before all this happened.

The phones were ringing off the hook, but neither Hector nor Maritza paid attention. Finally, Hector pushed a mute button on the console, which turned off the sound. They continued to watch as the star reverted to its previous form. Hector said something, almost to himself, as they watched the wonder unfolding before them. Maritza could barely hear it, but the words were unmistakable. "'...for we have seen his star in the east, and are come to worship him.'"

"Could this be similar to what the shepherds saw that night in Bethlehem?" she thought to herself. She couldn't be certain, of course, but, somehow, it gave her great comfort to think so.

"Let's go outside, Hector. I want to see the stars," Maritza took her husband's hand. Together they walked outside.

Sounds of the tropical night surrounded them as they stepped outside. It was a clear night. Humidity still hung in the air from an early evening shower. The Moon shining and in the distance reflected off the eastern side of the Andes. How often, Hector wondered, had the Incas stared into the heavens waiting for their gods to return? Perhaps they'd been here tonight. Now they could rest in peace, Their mission finally accomplished.

"Look at the stars, honey," Maritza said, as they stared into the Milky Way above. "Where is Sirius?"

Hector pointed to the brightest star in the southern sky. As they held each other closely, staring at the universe around them, a feeling of contentment embraced them both.

After awhile, Maritza said softly, "Honey, weren't we doing something in your office before all this started?"

Hector smiled at his beautiful wife. "I do believe you're right." They headed back inside. As they passed the monitor, Sirius twinkled on the screen.

CHAPTER XV

REVELATION

As Jose walked closer to the light, he could see that he was not alone. Other villagers, also attracted, were moving that way also. As word spread, people from all over the island, including the tourists at the hotels, were making their way toward Rano Raraku Quarry where the beam of light appeared to be directed.

Walking toward the light, Jose's two older sons joined him, with Carlos, Rosalita and Corazon trailing behind. The two newborn lambs, seemingly mesmerized by the light, were nearly galloping ahead, as if they wanted, *needed*, to be there, too.

Approaching the quarry it appeared as if the entire population of the island, some 3500 people, were turning out.

None of these people could have known that, as they were gathering near the Rano Raraku Quarry on Rapa Nui, 2300 miles to the east, in Valparaiso, there was growing concern. For the past hour, all communication with Easter Island had been cut off. No radio, no satellite, no signals of any kind were being received—not even from ships in the vicinity, which previously had been coming in loud and clear. It was a complete mystery.

Nearing the quarry, Jose could see that the beam of light appeared to be concentrated on the site where *El Gigante* lay.

El Gigante, largest of all the moai on the island, lay prone, unfinished and untouched since the ancient Rapanui carvers abandoned it centuries before. When finished *El Gigante* would have been nearly seventy-two feet high with a weight of about 160 tons. It was assumed that work on the carving was stopped either because the statue was too large to move, or because the food supply ran out and the workers died off before they could finish it. In any event, the giant statue remained as a monument to its makers skill and ingenuity.

Now, bathed in the eerie starlight, the statue seemed to be alive.

As Jose followed the light beam up from the moai toward the star, he noticed something even more peculiar about the star, besides its extreme brightness. At first, it appeared as a tiny black dot in the middle of the brightest part of the star, but as Jose continued to observe, the dark spot grew larger until the star resembled a small version of a total eclipse, with a black center surrounded by a halo.

It was then that Jose realized that he was no longer looking at the star.

Slowly a ship descended, as if following the light beam down to Earth. As if hypnotized, all eyes were trained on the giant disk as it continued its slow, steady descent. There were no obvious lights, windows or hatches on the ship. Jose could see that it was metallic, but with a strange lustre or glow, which Jose had not seen before.

At an altitude of about 300 feet, the ship slowed its descent, stopped and hovered above the giant monolith and the spellbound crowd below. Except for a low humming sound, the silence was palpable. Even the lambs were still.

As the ship hovered above, what had previously been a star-lit night was now becoming hazy. In fact, Easter Island was now shrouded in a heavy cloud layer, and a dense fogbank surrounded the entire island, making visual observation impossible. Rapa Nui's isolation from the rest of the world was now complete.

With piercing brown eyes, Jose studied the spacecraft above. He strained to see if there were any markings on the side of the ship which might help to identify it. There on the side, he saw an emblem painted in black on the metal. It resembled a bird with its wings spread. Underneath the bird, there appeared to be writing of some kind, but the characters were unrecognizable. They resembled ancient glyphs carved in wood, found on the island, but Jose couldn't be sure. In any case, he couldn't translate them. No one could. The ancient writings were as much a mystery as the statues themselves.

Jose estimated the ship to be about 600 feet in diameter and perhaps 100 feet tall at the center. The ship remained motionless, and except for the hum, no other sounds emanated from the craft. The entire crowd, which by now must have included nearly everyone on the island, seemed drawn to the spectacle, as moths to a flame.

Jose was joined by his family. Corazon, his wife of nearly twenty years, stood beside him, as she had always done. Descended from the native Polynesians, her ancestors had settled on the island centuries ago, but the "old ways" had become lost and she had grown up as perplexed by the statues as everyone else. Who carved them? Why?

These questions were no longer a concern to her, or to the, other than for the tourist dollars they generated. The statues were here. The had always been here. They would always be here.

"They are like the clouds in the sky," she shrugged. "When you are surrounded by something all the time, you ignore it. Let the outsiders decide what they mean. For me it is enough to know that they are here. Someone long ago thought it is important enough to make them. Who are we to question it? I see the moon up in the sky. Does it really matter why it is there? Can I move it? Can I make it go away? No! Someone greater than I decided it should be there. Isn't that enough?"

Such pragmatism was hard to argue with.

Jose, on the other hand, had always been a dreamer. As a young boy, he often played among the moai. He would stare up at the stony, silent sentinels, wondering what they must be thinking. Surely, he thought, they must be thinking of something. At night, after herding the flocks, Jose would see them standing in the moonlight, gazing out to sea, or facing inland, as if waiting for something to happen.

Now, perhaps, something was.

What would this mean for Jose? For his wife and children? Why were he and his family, and some of the others, *not* afraid to be here? Where could they go if they were afraid? What would become of the lives they had made here? What was the significance of the two newborn lambs, born out of season? These questions raced through Jose's mind as he stared at the object.

The humming was getting louder. Jose could almost feel it. Wait-- he *was* feeling it. The ground was vibrating.

Huddling closer together, the family felt the earth starting to shake. Many, panicked by the rumbling, ran away, some screaming. Others, transfixed, remained steadfast. "How foolish," Jose said. "Where are they running to?"

"What's happening, Papa?" Carlos gripped his father's hand.

"It's all right, son." Jose reassured him. "I'm here."

The lambs seemed indifferent to the whole affair. As the vibration increased, there appeared to a soft glow emanated from *El Gigante*. The vibration increased to a steady rumble. More people fled. The glow grew brighter. As it did, the glow of the spacecraft likewise increased. Suddenly, there was a huge cracking noise, as if boulders were breaking apart. Still more people fled, but Jose and his family remained.

"Look!" Carlos pointed to the statue. A definite crack had appeared between the unfinished moai and the surrounding rock. Light appeared to be coming from within the crack.

"It's moving!" Corazon fell to her knees. The others quickly followed. "Praise be to God!"

Slowly at first, the great stone monolith began to move vertically and horizontally, from its resting place. Light shone brightly from the site as the statue slowly moved away.Once clear, the head end of the carving began to rise.

"It's standing up!" Jose shouted. "Good God in heaven! It's standing up!"

He watched in awe as the giant statue slowly became vertical. At seventy-two feet high, and weighing nearly 165 tons, the huge stone figure was now floating in air about ten feet above the quarry, glowing nearly as bright as the giant yellow-orange disk above it.

For a few moments, the statue hung in midair. Then slowly it lowered to the ground, as the glow decreased and vibrations diminished.

Once the statue stood vertically and perpendicular to the ground its glow disappeared entirely, and the vibrations gave way to the humming present when the disk initially descended. Jose remembered what other islanders had said earlier, when asked by scientists how the ancients had moved the statues from the quarry and raised them in place on the ahu. "They walked," was their answer. "Ridiculous!" the scientists scoffed. Ridiculous, indeed.

The silent stone giant now stood beside the quarry and stared at the remainder of the assembly. Some had returned after their initial panic. Curiosity, Jose observed, could be a powerful force.

Some huddled in groups, while others could be heard mumbling prayers.

Aside from the humming, complete silence had returned. No wind whispered in the cloud filled sky, as Jose and his family stood up to look around.

An intense, white light shone upward from the former resting place of the giant moai. It bathed the underside of the hovering spacecraft, which had reverted to its original metallic lustre.

The two lambs, that had been so passive throughout the spectacle, pawed the Ground and bleated continuously. Romping, they moved toward the light. Carlos wanted to retrieve them, but his father held him back.

"Let them go, Carlos," he said, softly, holding his son's shoulders.

"Why, Papa?"

"It's God's will, my son," Jose replied, not quite believing what he had just said.

As the two lambs approached the light, a portal opened on the underside of the ship. It opened much like the iris of an eye, yet Jose was certain there were no seams on the disk's metallic skin.

The white light beaming upward from grotto, was now shining up through the portal, which Jose estimated to be about thirty feet in diameter. This light was joined by a bluish-white light which shone down from the portal into the depression. The young ram, Arturo took a position to the right of the grotto and laid down. He seemed perfectly at ease. The ewe, Rosalita, approached the light and stepped down into the grotto. Immediately upon doing so, a blinding flash of light ascended into the portal. Rosalita disappeared.

"Jose, come closer!" A deep, masculine voice spoke. "Come forward toward the light."

Startled by the sound, Jose glanced over his shoulder.

"Jose, come closer," the voice repeated.

Jose realized he was not the only one hearing the voice. Everyone else was looking around, too.

"Did you hear that?" Jose asked his wife.

"Yes," she said, "but I don't know where she is coming from."

"She?" Jose replied. "It was a man's voice I heard."

"No!" Corazon insisted, "it was a woman—soft and gentle. She said, "Corazon, come closer, toward the light."

"Jose," the voice repeated, "bring your family, too."

Jose looked at his wife and at his children. Without speaking, they walked toward the light, for as awesome as this power was, there was no feeling of malevolence. There was more a feeling of comfort, much like one experiences when returning home after a long journey.

As Jose looked up, he felt as if he were seeing a door standing open in heaven. The same voice he had heard earlier said, "Come up here and I will show you what must come in the future!"

Jose and is family were enveloped in a soft, white light. All else became whiteness. A mist filled the entire area surrounding them, and except for themselves, they could see nothing—no walls, no floor, no ceiling. However, unlike fog, this mist contained no moisture. Had theybeen brought aboard the ship, or had they been transported somewhere else? One thing *was* clear. This was not Rapa Nui.

As he stood in rapt silence within the mist, ever so gradually a form began to emerge in front of them. At first it appeared as a solid whiteness within the vaporous whiteness, but finally he was able to perceive the form of a large white chair. Some kind of form was seated upon it, but the figure was shrouded in mist.

Slowly, a ring of whiteness surrounding the chair began to emerge. It gradually transformed into twenty-four smaller white chairs, forming a ring around the larger one. As with the first chair, these were likewise occupied, but, also like the first, their forms were shrouded by the mist. Light streamed upward from behind the large chair now, and Jose counted six other light beams shining upward from behind the twenty-four smaller ones, which tended to divide the ring into six groups of four.

As he gazed into the light, Jose noticed other forms slowly taking shape. Above the large chair, he could see four shields come into view. The first resembled a lion's head. The second shield, to the right of the first, was an ox. To the right of the ox was a shield with a human face on it, and to the right of that one Jose saw one with an eagle, its wings spread as if in flight. It reminded him of the emblem he had seen on the side of the ship.

From the placement of the chairs, it was clear that whomever, or whatever occupied the first chair was the leader. Not only was it larger, but there were lights of white, red and green flashing around it, but the fog or mist prevented clearer observation. The smaller chairs had no flashing lights.

To Jose, it appeared as if the beings in the twenty-four chairs were somehow in communication with the being in the large one, but he could not hear anything. Corazon gripped her husband's hand, as Jose gripped his young son's right shoulder. The other three children stood immediately behind them, holding each other's hands. There was absolute silence. It was as if they found themselves within a holy place, and one did not speak in the presence of the Lord.

As the twenty-four beings continued to exchange communication with the larger one, Jose noticed that the larger one seemed either to have, or to be holding something on its right side. Like everything else, it, too was white, and from Jose's perspective it resembled a wand. Perhaps it was a remote control of some kind, but it was impossible to tell in this confounded mist.

Then, as Jose watched, to his left, and immediately to the right of the large chair, a fifth shield began to glow. Through the light, in absolutely white perfection, apprared the face of a lamb.

"Rosalita!" Carlos cried out. Jose clamped a hand over his son's mouth and whispered sternly in his ear, "Quiet!" The lamb's face did resemble that of Rosalita, and seemed to be looking at Jose as if it knew him. "How could this be?" Jose thought.

The wand held by the being in the large chair, swung to touch the lamb's face. Upon doing so, the lamb's face glowed brighter, and so did theshield of the lion. Above and behind the large chair, images appeared in the whiteness. At first they were vague, but as they continued to dance in the mist, they became clearer. There were scenes of battles. Ships fired guns. Planes dropped bombs. Cities were burning. There was destruction everywhere. A knight, mounted on a white steed gave a signal, Soldiers charged across a field, only to be met by withering arrows. There were scenes of explosions, culminating in the detonation of an atomic bomb. The sounds were deafening.

Then, it stopped.

The wand touched the lamb again. Again it glowed, but this time followed by the shield with the ox. New images appeared. Scenes of anarchy and revolution filled the void. Old statues were pulled down, flags waved in the air, and riots filled the streets. There was shouting and screaming, with sounds of gunshot. Visions of the guillotine and firing squads now flashed before them. Corazon covered her eyes. Little Carlos, now crying, buried his face in his father's arms as a soldier, mounted on a red horse, rode through the crowds slashing with his bayonet.

Again it stopped.

When the wand touched the lamb for the third time, the shield with the man's faced glowed.Famine, and disease, and funeral pyres laid fields to waste. An emaciated black horse pawed at the ground, desperately searching for food. Starving children filled hospitals along with the sick and dying, the weeping and the crying. Corazon and Rosalita were now crying uncontrollably, while Juan and Pablo turned their heads in shame. Unable to control himself any longer, Jose lashed out, "Why do you punish us so?"

No answer came as the third series of images ended.

Once again the wand touched the lamb's face, and the shield of the eagle glowed. It Soared above the Earth, as if an in flight. Rows of white crosses littered the fields—cemeteries of the uncounted dead. In the distance, a lone soldier mounted on a pale horse, played taps as another body was laid to rest. Again the eagle soared into the sky, above the killing fields below—the battlefields and the death camps with the moaning of the injured and the dying—as Jose shuddered, sick with grief.

Finally, the images stopped. Jose and his family again fell to their knees before this power which surrounded them. Except for the tearful sobbing of Jose's family there was now complete silence again. The mist continued to shroud them. Jose considered what he had just seen, frightful images—images of war, and of anarchy—of famine, and of death. Images of man against man had passed in front of him—images of man against—himself!

Jose slowly lifted his head. The wand touch the lamb again.

A voice spoke. Its words were clear and unmistakable, as it said, "All this we have given you. See what you have become." This was followed by a cacophony of voices which built to a deafening roar. Jose's entire family covered their ears. It was as if suddenly all the souls who had ever trod the Earth were crying out together. "Crying out for what?" Jose shouted through the din.

"For justice," the voice answered, and silence instantly returned.

For a sixth time, the wand touched the lamb, and for a sixth time visions appeared, terrible scenes of earthquakes, tidal waves and storms. Meteorites crashed into the earth. The sun went dark, as men ran to escape from the wrath of nature.

Again the voice spoke, "Use what has been given you wisely, or this will be your fate. In seven days the earth was created, and with seven plagues it can be destroyed. The first will be fire, to burn all the forests and grain. The second will be earthquakes and tidal waves to destroy man's ships and coastlines. The third will be a giant meteorite crashing into the Earth, causing mass destruction throughout the world. The sun will be covered by dust, leading to the fourth plague, as darkness covering the Earth, killing most of the animals and plants. The fifth plague will be an epidemic of disease, causing agony among much of the remaining population. This will lead to the sixth plague of war and annihilation."

After a brief pause the voice continued, devoid of emotion. "The few survivors of these six plagues must then endure the seventh."

Jose was too afraid to ask, but curiosity forced him to, "And what is that?" he asked.

"The few who survive will be transported to a new colony," the voice replied, "a new world, where the process will begin again. There are no failures in the universe—merely occasional disappointments," the voice said.

"Now go, and take this message to all the people. Tell them of what you have seen here. Tell them that they must use the gifts they have been given for the benefit of all mankind. The possibilities are endless.

In a breath, the light was gone.

Jose looked around him. Just as quickly as he had left, he was back on Rapa Nui. The giant disk rose above the island, heading back into the brightness of Sirius. Anxiously—joyfully, he hugged his wife and children. "did you hear it?" he shouted.

"Yes," Corazon replied, "I heard every word she spoke."

"She?" Jose asked, puzzled again by his wife's response. "And what about you?" He asked his children.

"Yes, we heard, Papa," his children replied in unison.

Eager to know if other Easter Islanders had seen and heard what he did, Jose shouted, "Did you see it? Were you in the light?"

"Yes," came the reply.

The ship had nearly disappeared from view, and it appeared as if the brightness of the star had begun to diminish. The clouds had lifted and the starlit night reappeared. All was silence as the people wondered at the giant stone statue, now erect before them. a silent reminder of what they had witnessed this night.

As they watched the giant monolith standing in the now starlit sky, there came the bleating of a lamb.

"Arturo!" Carlos yelled. He ran to the young ram and held it in his arms. Indifferent to all the excitement of the evening, the lamb continued to bleat. "Papa,?" Carlos asked. Where is Rosalita?"

Jose paused for a moment, and looked up toward the star. "She is there, son," he said slowly, as he continued to look up. "She's up there—in a better place."

As Carlos hugged his young ram, a voice suddenly cried out, "Over here! Come quickly! You must see this!"

Jose, his family, and many of the other islanders ran over to the depression, or grotto, where *El Gigante* had been.

What they saw there filled them with hope and wonder. In the bottom of the depression was a large golden chest, covered with ornate engravings, and with handles on both ends. On the top of the chest two eagles faced each other with wings spread, similar to the one Jose had seen on the ship.

"They must have left it here," someone said.

"No," Jose replied. "They didn't leave it here. They were returning it."

* * *

Back in Spring Valley, Patty had finished her bath. Contentment and joy had swept over her ever since her conversation with Jonas. Pouring herself a glass of Frangelica on the rocks she stepped out onto the terrace. It was a clear night here as well. Staring into the heavens, she raised her glass and gave a silent toast. Here's to the new day, she thought. She sipped her drink. "Tomorrow I'm going to call Hector," she said to the stars. "He'll never believe *this*."